BE

KU-222-262

A SHADOW ON THE WALL

A SHADOW ON THE WALL

Jonathan Aycliffe

This first world edition published in Great Britain 2000 by
SEVERN HOUSE PUBLISHERS LTD of
9–15 High Street, Sutton, Surrey SM1 1DF.
This first world edition published in the U.S.A. 2000 by
SEVERN HOUSE PUBLISHERS INC of
595 Madison Avenue, New York, N.Y. 10022.

British Library Cataloguing in Publication Data

Aycliffe, Jonathan, 1949-
   A shadow on the wall
   1.Demonology - Fiction 2.Horror tales
   I. Title
   823.9'14 [F]

   ISBN 0-7278-5505-0

Typeset by Palimpsest Book Production Ltd
Polmont, Stirlingshire, Scotland
Printed and bound in Great Britain by
MPG Books Ltd, Bodmin, Cornwall.

Acknowledgements

My thanks to all those who, in their various ways, smoothed the way to my completing this new exercise in traditional terror, above all my wife, Beth, for her unswerving support and love, my agent, Giles Gordon, for his wisdom and persistence, and Patricia Parkin, for her early thoughts on the text.

To Beth, may her shadow never fade.

One

A therton appeared in my rooms two or three days after my accident. He had heard about it from Burridge, which means the news must have travelled round most of Cambridge by then. By 'Cambridge', I mean, of course, the university.

I did not know Matthew Atherton especially well, and it surprised me to find him there, all of a dither because he had forgotten something or other, a look of concern on his ample features.

"My hat," he mumbled, "I seem to have come out without my hat."

He belonged to one of the smaller colleges, and we had had little occasion to cross paths in the past. A shared interest in books, an occasional dinner party in the rooms of a fellow don, a chance encounter at a public lecture of mutual interest had, until that afternoon, been the sum total of our familiarity, if such it may be called.

Atherton is a curious-looking man, corpulent, yet almost dainty in his mannerisms. His features, which one would expect to be coarse in a man of such girth, are rather fine, if they do not, indeed, verge on the angelic, and his eyes seem to peer out from his face as if to say, "I am a prisoner in a body not truly my own." I cannot say I altogether like him, I would not go so far as that, but I confess to a certain admiration for him. He is aged somewhere between thirty-five and forty – I have not been able to ascertain the exact year of his birth – and is the son of respectable parents from Lincolnshire. His father was Bishop of Ely and, I believe, a man of learning in his own right.

Speaking of which, I have not mentioned Atherton's exceptional erudition. It was that which sparked my first interest, the day he called, for I knew him to have the reputation of one of the cleverest men in the university, and I found it strange to find him so much at a loss in my company.

Atherton is a Fellow of Sidney Sussex, at which college he has taught Greek for several years. My acquaintances tell me, however, that he is very much the leading man in this country in the science of philology (if science it can be called). Apart from the classical languages, he is reputed to be entirely fluent in Sanskrit and ancient Egyptian, and to be competent in both ancient and modern Persian (which he studied with Browne at Pembroke). He is proficient in Arabic, Hebrew, and Aramaic. French, German, Italian, and Russian he reads easily, and he 'gets by' in Spanish and Portuguese.

But linguistic skills are but a fraction of Atherton's abilities. He sat for the mathematics tripos in the year following his Classics degree, and emerged Senior Wrangler of 1871. He was then only twenty. His knowledge of Greek mathematics is unsurpassed, and he has extended his interests to the Indian and Muslim systems, being the only mathematician of note to have a mastery of the native languages in which all the essential texts are to be found. Burton tells me he has published numerous papers and studies of the Arabic translations of Archimedes' *Stomachion* and *Lemmata*. All this in a man of between thirty-five and forty!

But these observations are by the by. They serve as a sort

2

of introduction to Atherton and his personality, above all to alert the reader to his being a man of science as much as one of letters. He and I have since become – not exactly friends, for we are not of like temperament, but, shall we say, close acquaintances. How this came about, I shall presently relate.

He stood hatless in my room that day – it was a cold afternoon in December, and snow had begun to fall across the court – blinking as though the sight of my leg in bandages disconcerted him, as well it might. I had slipped some days earlier on an icy path in Trumpington Street, fracturing my right ankle, and was now confined indefinitely to my rooms in King's. Atherton brought with him the sound of singing, for the choir were just then practising for the Advent service, and my rooms are in the chapel end of the Gibb's Building.

"I heard . . ." he began, and dried up at once. He is something of a recluse, and I do not think he had ever visited the sick before. For my own part, I was racking my brains to place him more accurately. An embarrassing silence ensued, he standing disconsolate, I scanning his features for a clue as to why he of all people should turn up in my rooms like this.

"Please," I said, "take a chair."

His clothes were damp from the snow, and small fragments of white, now melting, still clung to his unruly hair.

He sat and continued to look at me mutely, like a newly arrived undergraduate bereft of the powers of conversation.

"Will you take a sherry?" I asked. It was four in the afternoon, and I never normally touch any form of drink until I set foot in the Senior Common Room on my way to dine in hall; but I reckoned that being an invalid has its compensations, and Atherton did appear in need of something to warm him.

"You'll find a bottle in that cupboard," I went on, pointing to the corner, "and some glasses."

He nodded mildly and fetched the sherry without a murmur. His hand trembled slightly as he poured a measure into each glass. I was wondering what on earth to say to him. I am an historian, and though I have a tolerable knowledge of the Classics and one or two European languages, I did not think myself capable of following Atherton in an abstruse discussion of the higher realms of philology. As for mathematics, I fear I have never scaled its precipitous heights, indeed I count myself fortunate if I can add up my tailor's bill.

My fears were rapidly dispersed. He sat watching me for several minutes, taking an occasional nervous sip of sherry, as though steeling himself for some revelation or impertinence. The sound of choral voices drifted through thickening snow and thence through my window, enveloping me in the goodwill of the season. Botts had lit my lights, and had promised to return later with supper on a tray. I had almost let my eyes close, the better to enjoy the music, when Atherton found courage to speak.

"It's not for myself," he faltered. "I've come about my brother, the Reverend Edward Atherton. You may have heard of him."

I shook my head. He nodded distractedly and went on.

"Edward is my older brother. He came under my father's influence a great deal in his youth, and in consequence entered the Church. To be perfectly honest, he was never really suited to the ecclesiastical life. His deepest inclinations are artistic, and he has never had the ambition to seek preferment. Our father found Edward something of a disappointment. For all that, he is well liked by his parishioners. I do believe he is a good man, and that must count for something, must it not?"

He gave me a look of the most disarming innocence, all the more accentuating that angelic quality I had already marked in his features. I nodded my assent, and, with a smile that quickly faded, he recommenced his account of his brother.

"Edward is now the rector at Thornham St Stephen, out beyond March. I don't know if you've heard of it?"

Something came to mind, though I could not then have said quite what. A faint memory of a passage read in a gazetteer, or a reference in a local history. An event during the Reformation, perhaps.

"The name is familiar, of course. But I can't say I . . ."

"No, of course not, it's not a particularly important place, quite insignificant, in fact, and the church is not very remarkable. Though, to an antiquarian such as yourself . . ." He paused, as if uncertain what interest an antiquarian might find in his brother's church.

"Quite," I said, trying to be as encouraging as possible. It had just came back to me that the church at Thornham St Stephen was outstanding. I noticed that he had set down his sherry as though fearful it might interfere with his train of thought. For my own part, I wondered where this was leading.

"It is not exactly on a matter of antiquarian interest that I have come here," he went on, "although I think that may come into it. I have heard . . ." He seemed uneasy, and I began to have an inkling of what he might be aiming at. "That is, one or two of my friends have told me that you have an interest in matters . . . shall we say, supernatural."

He halted, as though embarrassed by what he had just said, and looked at me with a most pitiable expression in his eyes. Now, all was clear; but there was something in his look I did not like, something that chilled me. Atherton had not come on a trivial errand. Whatever troubled him must be very serious indeed.

"I would prefer to speak of psychic phenomena," I answered. "It is the preferred term among those of us who take a scientific interest in these matters."

"Then you are not a believer?"

I hesitated, as I always do when challenged on this point.

"I would describe myself as an open-minded sceptic," I said. "And you?"

"Oh, I . . ." He reddened and looked away, staring at the snow as it drifted past my window. I had asked Botts to leave the curtains open: I found it hard enough to be confined without being shut in altogether.

He turned his troubled gaze back to me.

"I was a thorough sceptic," he said, "and even now . . . Yet, if you had seen my brother, heard what he has to say . . . The fact is, my scepticism is all in shreds, and I must have help."

"Whatever is the matter?" I asked. My concern for him was growing every moment. He was shivering, though the temperature in my rooms was far from low. "Are you unwell?"

He shook his head.

"A slight chill," he said. "But I am greatly disturbed in mind. My brother— The truth is, I think he may be going out of his mind, indeed I fear for his life. You must help him. I beg of you."

"Surely a physician . . ."

He shook his head quite violently, as though I had blasphemed.

"A physician would be useless, worse than useless. As for an alienist . . ."

"No, of course not, I did not suggest that he is actually mad."

"It has been suggested. My mother has said as much. She thinks Edward should travel to Geneva or Vienna. Ever since our father became ill, she has been the force in the family. But I have defied her in this. Edward is troubled in his spirit, not his mind. That is why I have come to you, and not to any physician."

I shifted, feeling trapped by the bandages at the end of my leg. In the room above mine, Morgan was pacing back and forth, as he often did when wrestling with some intractable problem in logic.

"I really don't think this falls within my sphere at all," I said, imbuing my voice with as much regret and sympathy as I could muster for someone I scarcely knew. "Would your brother not be better advised to speak with his bishop, or whoever it is rectors consult in matters of the spirit?"

This latest suggestion elicited an even more violent reaction than that preceding it. Atherton jumped to his feet and walked about agitatedly for some time before returning, somewhat more self-possessed, to his chair.

"I apologise," he said. "You do not know me, and here I am in your inner sanctum, behaving like some sort of madman. What you must think of me, I can scarcely guess. Perhaps you will imagine that it is I, and not my brother, who requires the services of an alienist."

I shook my head in disavowal, yet I must own that I had already formulated much that same doubt in my own mind. Atherton was, after all, a virtual stranger, and nothing I had heard of his character had predisposed me to think of him as a fully balanced man.

"The fact is," he continued, "that my brother will not breathe a word about his troubles to his bishop. The Bishop of Ely reckons himself a rationalist, and he is particularly sharp in his criticism of anyone dabbling in mediumistic seances or anything of that character. He will not have it that the spirits of the dead may remain earthbound, and he regards the rite of exorcism as a popish heresy. It is quite out of the question for my brother to approach him, or indeed any of the senior clergy, on this matter."

"And what exactly is this matter?" I asked.

Atherton remained silent. Beyond my windows, beyond the snow, beyond the darkness binding us in, the voices of the choristers celebrated the coming birth of the Christ child. A shiver passed through me, as one had passed through Atherton earlier. I felt a sense of foreboding, a growing conviction that Atherton had not come to me on trivial business, that something dark lay at the bottom of his visit.

"There is a very great evil at work in my brother's church," he said. "Edward thinks . . . He is certain that he has disturbed something that should have been allowed to rest." He fell silent again.

"Can you be more precise?" I asked him. "What, precisely, has happened at Thornham St Stephen?"

Two

"It all started about four months ago," he began. I watched him carefully as he spoke, as interested in the man as in his story. He spoke slowly, pausing to choose his words and phrases, uncertain of their possible impact on me – a linguist shipwrecked on the rocks of his own tongue.

"The church at Thornham St Stephen is one of the finest in the region, but much neglected on account of its surroundings, which are indifferent, and its position in a remote part of the fens, in the Isle of Ely. The main building dates from the fourteenth century: the foundations were laid in the reign of Edward II. But there is evidence of earlier structures. The crypt is Norman, and some graves date back to the eighth century."

"Of course," I said. "I do remember reading of it in Lyson's *Magna Britannia*."

"Ah, then you may also remember that St Stephen's is possessed of several notable features, among which is to be numbered a group of tombs built in the fourteenth and fifteenth centuries. One consequence of the village's remoteness was that it survived the Reformation and the Commonwealth with its treasures intact and its fabric undamaged. Cromwell's Roundheads never set foot there, and it still boasts the statuary and figurative ornamentation with which it was originally endowed.

"This is especially gratifying in the case of the largest tomb, a marble structure built in 1359 for one William de Lindesey. De Lindesey was at one time prior of a small religious house at Thornham St Stephen, when it was a dower church of Thornham Abbey. In later life, William himself became Abbot of Thornham. He left instructions in his will that he was to be buried in the chancel of St Stephen's, together with large sums of money for the construction of the tomb and prayers for his soul.

"It's a fine example of a parish-church tomb of that period, one of the finest in the country, I understand. But, if the Roundheads spared it, the years have not been kind. Many of its figures are eroded, and large cracks have appeared in the sides.

"This summer, my brother, who had been given the living at Thornham St Stephen about a twelvemonth before, determined to remedy the very evident dilapidation he saw throughout the church. I have mentioned, I think, that Edward is of an artistic temperament. He draws exquisitely, and has made quite a study of the churches in his region, making sketches of their most distinctive features.

"I should explain that Edward has been a member of the Ecclesiological Society since his student days at Cambridge. You are familiar with its work, of course?"

I was indeed familiar with the society and its traditionalist principles, with which I am in little sympathy. It was founded here in Cambridge as the Camden Society about fifty years ago, a clique of enthusiasts who wish to return the nation's churches to what they consider their true medieval style. They are fussy High Church people, rather too fond of incense and candles, vestments and altar frontals for my somewhat simple taste.

I nodded.

"Edward used to contribute articles to *The Ecclesiologist*, some of them quite learned pieces. Of course, he's not much of a scholar – he lacks the necessary patience and application. But when he tries he can produce work of a tolerable quality. You may even have read some of his articles yourself. There was one on the subject of misericords that I found diverting."

I shook my head wearily.

"I fear *The Ecclesiologist* was never a journal I read. That sort of thing is . . . hardly to my taste."

"But you are an antiquarian."

"Of course. But that doesn't mean I wish to live in the Middle Ages."

He smiled awkwardly.

"Indeed, no. I should hate that myself. But Edward would disagree most strongly with you. Indeed he would. He is most vehement in his admiration for that period, most vehement. St Stephen's was an ideal church for him, of course. When the living became vacant, he actually wrote to the dean to ask for it. The church is like any other, it has been altered over the years, and its furnishings are far from the Society's Gothic ideal. Nevertheless, it has retained more of its original features than most, and my brother considered it a worthy object for his attentions. Of course, the bishop gave the project his blessing."

"Another Ecclesiologist?"

He smiled faintly and nodded.

"But, of course. They're all 'pals', you know. Even so, there was the usual question about where the money for the restoration would come from, but Edward has a small private income, and he was able to persuade the diocese that the work could be accomplished without calling on much-needed funds. He decided to begin by restoring the chancel, since that is the most sacred part of the church. The most prominent feature of the chancel at St Stephen's is the de Lindesey tomb. My brother set to work on it the very day the bishop authorised the undertaking."

Atherton paused, as though his fund of words had suddenly run low. There was a ravaged look in his pale eyes, and I noticed how he passed his hands one across the other, as though he washed them. Some inner torment gnawed at the man. I had misgivings as to where this was leading.

"I do not know quite what happened," he continued, "for Edward has veiled over the precise train of events in the accounts he has given me. I have gathered that work on the tomb was extensive, and that it involved dismantling most of the structure in order to restore its foundations. Of what took place there he will not speak, though I understand he was present all the time the work was proceeding.

"It is my impression that the masons disturbed something they should not have in the course of their labours. During the work one of the workmen had a serious accident, as a result of which he lost a leg and eventually died. A few days later, another was struck down by a fever, and in spite of the best efforts of the local doctor he also died within three days.

"Since then my brother has been a changed man. Work on the church has stopped, and he says it will not recommence. At first, I thought Edward's condition no more than a reaction to the shock of seeing two men die within such a short space of time, but as time passes I am confident it is more than that."

"What precisely do you mean?"

"I don't know for certain. All I can tell you is that he has fallen seriously ill. For months now, he has scarcely slept at night. When I enquired, I was told that he will not go to bed without a light. He is an unmarried man, and sleeps alone. On those few occasions I have stayed with him of late, he has entreated me to share his room at night. Wakeful myself, I have noticed that he starts as if at sudden sounds, when there are none. I catch him staring as though he can see something, but when I look there is nothing to be seen. Otherwise, he is of sound mind. His doctor says he can detect nothing physically wrong, yet he fears for Edward's life should this continue. I beseech you to help him. You are the only hope he has."

I was bewildered by this account, so full was it of generalities and vague allusions. There could be any number of reasons for Edward Atherton's lamentable condition.

"I regret I am not a physician," I said. "I don't see how I could possibly be of assistance to your brother."

He shook his head vehemently, more vehemently than seemed proper in a man blessed with such a cherubic countenance.

"It is not a physician I seek," he said, his voice quite thick with emotion. "It is not a physical ailment that threatens my brother's life. His body may be in danger, but I believe it is his mortal soul that is most truly at peril."

"Then I really cannot be of assistance. I am not a clergyman, indeed I am not even a believer," I protested. I was wishing he would leave. The conversation was vexing me.

Atherton got to his feet, angered by my deliberate obtuseness.

"You are trifling with me," he said angrily. "I have already told you that this is not a clerical matter, that the Church authorities would have nothing to do with it. My brother requires the services of someone who understands whatever forces these may be that are destroying him. I ask you again: are you willing to help, or must I leave Edward to his fate?"

His voice had changed from anger to dread, and I found myself dismayed both by his evident concern for his brother's well-being and by the clear distress my behaviour had caused him.

"Please," I urged, "try not to distress yourself. Sit down and tell me exactly what it is you wish me to do. I make no promises, but I will at least listen to you."

He hesitated, drawing a hand over his head and face, dislodging strands of wispy hair. His agitation communicated itself to me. I watched him nervously as he resumed his seat.

"Here," he said. "Perhaps this will help explain what it is I seek from you."

He drew a piece of crumpled pale blue paper from his pocket and passed it to me without another word. When I glanced at it, I saw nothing but lines of scribbled writing, jotted down in purple ink as though in haste. Both sides of the sheet were covered in the fine, spidery writing.

"I'm sorry," I said, "but I don't understand what this is."

"It's a page from a diary of sorts," he answered. "My brother has been keeping it. He has a large Bible which he carries with him at all times. At night, he lies in bed – I do not say 'he sleeps' – with it beneath his pillow. In the middle of a conversation, he will break off in order to leaf through it, in search of some passage or other. The habit is a new one, formed only in recent months.

"He keeps little sheets of paper like this interleaved with the pages of the text. At first I thought them notes he kept there to use in his sermons, or perhaps to help in writing his commentary on the Pauline Epistles, on which he has been working for several years. But one day about two weeks ago, while I was there on a visit, this leaf fell from the book without his noticing. I only caught sight of it later, when he was no longer in the room, and I picked it up, meaning to return it to him. But when I saw what it was, I slipped it into my pocket instead, thinking it might serve as an indication of my poor brother's state of mind."

I looked again at the little sheet. Bit by bit, I succeeded in deciphering Edward Atherton's rapid, nervous hand. I still have the sheet in my desk drawer, and am able to reproduce some of it here.

September 4th

Prayed alone in the chancel this evening. He was laughing all the time I stayed there, until I could stand it no more and left. As I returned to the nave, I saw his shadow on the pulpit.

September 15th

Sive irascatur sive rideat non inveniet requiem. 'Whether he rage or laugh, there is no rest.'

Friday

Considerat peccator iustum. 'The wicked watcheth the right-eous.' I saw him twice today, once in the chancel, and again in the parvis, where I had gone to read. He did not laugh, but remained silent and watched me. I pretend to ignore him, but he knows it is a front. Where is my Saviour? I pray, but the heavens remain closed, as though a lock had been placed there.

I have written again to my lord bishop, pleading he set things right; but I look for little help from that quarter. What have I done?

October 5th

One of the choirboys has been taken ill, young Will Manning. I visited him today, but could not stay long. I had no words of comfort for his parents, who are frightened he may die like Thomas Rawlings, whose symptoms were similar. I have spent the afternoon in prayer, but I have little hope. Dear God, I may yet have to perform the exorcism myself.

October 6th

Si quis tetigerit os illius vel sepulchrum inmundus erit. 'Whoseoever toucheth a bone of a man, or a grave, shall be unclean.'

I looked up to find Atherton gazing at me anxiously. When I handed the paper back to him, his hand was all of a flutter.

"This does indeed make things clearer," I said. "But you should understand that it is perfectly possible your brother has been suffering hallucinations."

"I was not given to understand that you were a sceptic."

I shook my head.

"I am. But I am by no means rigid. Such things as are described in your brother's notes are possible. I do not dismiss them out of hand. But as often as not there are other explanations. Fraud (which I consider out of the question here), misreporting, natural phenomena, and hallucination. I can rule nothing out without fuller evidence."

"But you will look for such evidence?"

I hesitated, but inwardly I knew I was beaten. He gave me no choice.

"If you would like me to do so, yes. But you see how things are with me. My doctor has given me strict orders to remain in bed for at least a week. I dare not set foot outside these rooms for a fortnight or more. Travelling to Thornham St Stephen is out of the question."

"My brother is a dying man."

"I recognise your urgency, Mr Atherton, but surely you see that I have no choice in the matter. I do promise, however, that the moment I am given permission to move, I shall be on my way to visit your brother."

"He may be dead by then."

"Then I suggest you find some means of preventing it. It is almost Christmas. Surely he will accept an invitation to spend the season with you here, or at your mother's house."

He looked doubtful, but agreed to try.

"I will let you know the moment I'm allowed to travel. If I come across anything that might shed light on the case, I'll write to you. And if you hear anything further, please don't hesitate to let me know."

"Very well," he said. I could see the disappointment etched on his face, and the resignation with which he stood and made for the door. As he reached it, he turned to me.

"I'll try to make him leave," he said, "but I don't hold out much hope. He won't abandon his parish for the Christmas season."

"Has he no curate?" I asked.

"Yes, of course – a man called Lethaby. I've met him once, but I can't say I took to him. A dry stick of a man, humourless and, I think, most ambitious. Edward would never leave the parishioners in his care at such a time."

"Then pray for him," I said. "You can do that, at least."

He looked at me, as though surprised to hear such advice from an unbeliever. In all honesty, I had said it for his comfort more than out of any conviction it would do any good. I had begun to fear the worst for his brother.

"Yes," he said, "I shall pray for him. But I do not think my prayers will be answered."

When he had gone, I lay in bed for a long time, listening to the voices of the choir at evensong. Outside, the darkness thickened and grew strange.

Three

In the event, I was less than true to my word. I did not get in touch with Atherton, I did not ask for books that might have told me more about Thornham St Stephen and its church, I did not even mention to Dr Phillips that I might want to travel out to the fens. Confined to my rooms, I spent my time propped up in bed or sitting in an armchair with my leg stretched out in front of me on an embroidered stool. I read and wrote as much as possible, and my friends were solicitous: they would pop in to keep me abreast of the latest university gossip or to go through neglected items of college business. My students resumed their tutorial visits, and I listened to their ill-formed essays almost eagerly for once, as though to blot out thoughts I would rather not have had.

But, in the end, colleagues and students alike would leave me to myself, and I would face long dull hours in which my thoughts returned again and again to the events at Thornham St Stephen.

In particular, I was troubled by those scriptural quotations with which Edward Atherton had interspersed his jottings, the meaning of which remained obscure to me. And I regretted not having asked the other Atherton what had been the fate of the choirboy who had fallen ill.

I had all but resolved to speak with Atherton again,

when Christmas intervened. My sister Agnes, who lives in Trumpington, arranged to have me stay at her home for most of the vacation. She is married to Napier, the Queens' Fellow who has made such a name for himself in biology of late. Charles is a kind man, and my sister appears to be entirely happy with him, though I am not sure she is ideally suited to be the wife of a don. Napier can be a little stuffy, and is often wrapped up in his research. He was one of the first college fellows to take advantage of the Revised Statutes that allowed them the comforts of the married state, but he did so rather late in life, and I am not sure he has adjusted well. The children are, I fear, something of a thorn in his academic flesh. Yet he mocks me for my own continued celibacy, and with Agnes's connivance endeavours – I may say without success – to present me with a string of eligible spinsters, none of them remotely suited to me.

Not many of us in Cambridge keep carriages. The colleges are all within walking distance of one another, and most academics continue to reside in rooms. The question of how I might be transported exercised us all terribly at first. My brother-in-law keeps a horse, but that was hardly a suitable conveyance for one in my condition. In the end Dr Phillips arranged for me to be taken to Trumpington in his brougham, and my vacation was saved.

I had such a delightful time with Agnes and her family that time quite slipped away. This year I was mercifully spared the parade of spinsters. Perhaps I should sprain my ankle more often.

It was well past New Year when I finally returned to college, many pounds heavier and with a lighter mind. I scarcely thought of the Athertons all the time I stayed at Trumpington. Imagine my consternation, therefore, when the porter brought me a message which had been waiting for me since Christmas Eve, marked 'Urgent' and bearing the crest of Sidney Sussex on the rear of the envelope.

The letter was from Atherton, and in it he reproached me for not having got in touch. He was about to set off for Thornham St Stephen, having just learned that his brother's condition had deteriorated in the meantime. Would I please follow him there if at all possible, for he feared the worst. I surmised that it had not, after all, proved possible to dislodge Atherton from his church.

I immediately sent to Sidney Sussex, apologising for my lack of consideration, and asking Atherton to contact me at his first opportunity, indicating that I was still willing to lend what assistance I might to the efforts he was making in his brother's behalf.

Within the half-hour, Atherton appeared in my rooms in person, much altered since his last visit. His face, though it had lost little of its plumpness, seemed drawn, and his skin paler than it had been. Beneath their cherub's lids, his green eyes showed signs of strain.

I rose from my chair and, reaching for my stick, made to hobble towards him, but he hurried forward, pressing me back. He stood above me for a moment, his cheeks quivering.

"What's happened?" I asked.

"My brother is dead," he said. "I received a telegram an hour ago, and then your note. I hardly know what to do. I must go down, but I can't face it alone. Will you come with me?"

"Dead?" I echoed. "Did the telegram say what caused his death?"

Atherton shook his head.

"No, it was short and to the point. Lethaby sent it – Edward's curate. I've heard he is most economical."

20

"And have you answered him?"

He shook his head. His entire bearing bespoke despondency. He had not come to rebuke me but to seek my help. This time I could not in all conscience refuse it.

"You must telegraph to him at once," I said. "Tell him to expect us this evening. Perhaps he will do us the courtesy of reserving rooms for us at the local inn."

Four

We reached Thornham St Stephen a little before sunset, in time to see a tired and heavy sun drop down through ragged purple clouds. A dogcart had brought us out from March. It was a long and tedious journey, and my leg ached insufferably all the way. On all sides, the flat expanse of the fens stretched to infinity. We seemed marooned in a world unlike any other, in a landscape almost without feature, frosted, bleak, and white. Midwinter lay on the untidy fields like a penitential garment, ravaging and quite without pity. The dykes, filled with winter water and ice, ran in unbroken lines through the dark, knitting horizon to horizon. I saw a farmer walk, huddled and alone, in a wind-driven expanse where there was no habitation. The sound of our horse's hooves rang across the gaunt open countryside and was lost for ever among the marshes.

We saw the village long before we came to it across the flat surrounding wastes. It seemed to have no purpose, to be nothing more than a crouching of buildings set down in dead country. Before all else, we saw the church tower, lifted above the world like a tower of Babel, and as we approached a single bell began to toll, as though in anticipation of our coming, or as a warning of it.

The village, as we entered it, lay grey and forbidding at

the end of a long rutted lane. Our conveyance bounced and cracked its way along, unsettling us both, and sending jolts of pain through my leg. Low, unprepossessing cottages huddled together on either side of the track, their doors shut tight, their windows shuttered against the sharp fen winds. I saw a white face at a window, staring down at us briefly, then jerking back into the shadow in the room behind.

The Three Windmills had been named after a trio of local windpumps that serve to drain Thornham Fen into the Middle Level Drain. It was situated on a drab, winter-stained green, more frosted mud than grass. A weathered sign showing three faded mills hung crookedly above the door, and a faint light crept out onto the cobbled street. The dogcart driver deposited us and our luggage outside, and made off at once, a small lantern swinging at his stern like a diminishing star.

Atherton pushed open the door and helped me over the stoop into a hot candlelit room full of flickering shadows. The room was still and empty, and the only sound came from the tolling bell outside. Atherton stuck his head through a door at one side, but came back to say it too was empty. A fire was blazing in the hearth, and, from the look of it, it had been lit not very long before.

"Hello!" I called. "Is there anyone here?"

Atherton went back to the door and called through it. No one answered, but I heard footsteps somewhere above us, then the sound of quick steps on a stair.

Moments later, a ragged-looking girl appeared in the doorway. She took one look at us, gulped, tried to perform a curtsey, and disappeared as fast as she had come.

"The landlady is Mrs O'Reilly," Atherton said, moving across to the fire in order to warm his hands. "A local woman, in spite of the name. Her husband was an Irishman who came here to dig dykes and stayed to take over the inn. He died ten years ago, but she keeps the place on almost single-handed. No children. She will have been badly affected by Edward's death. Before his arrival, she stayed away from church, but she says he rekindled her faith, or some such thing."

"It's very cut off," I said, thinking of the long, dim drive and the raddled vastness of the landscape. "Why did your brother want to come here? Surely he could have had a better living elsewhere."

Atherton nodded.

"Indeed he could; but it wasn't in Edward's nature to seek the easy way. To tell you the truth, he was something of a recluse. He remained unmarried because the thought of family life filled him with horror. All he wanted to do was tend his parish and pursue his interests in the liturgy and medieval architecture. He was desperate to come here. The church was quite magnificent once, when it was a dependency of Thornham Abbey. Edward had the highest hopes for it."

At that moment, the door opened again and we were treated to the sight of a weeping woman, a soiled apron fast against her eyes, stumbling towards Atherton.

"Dr Atherton! Dr Atherton! What's to become of us? Rector dead and gone."

She reached for him, and he held her clumsily, consoling her as though it was her brother and not his that had died. But her tears, if maudlin, were genuine enough, and her grief as real as any sister's.

Slowly, by dint of repeated words of comfort, Atherton detached the little woman and guided her to a chair. He sat down beside her, and looked up, motioning to me to take a chair myself. I was already finding the strain of standing too great, and readily joined them.

Mrs O'Reilly blubbered a little longer, then subsided until her sobs were manageable. She was a solidly built woman of around fifty, well worn by hard labour, with a tanned face and tiny purple eyes made puffy from crying. From time to time, Atherton patted the back of her hand, but I could see he was not at ease in the role of comforter. And, after all, it was his brother who had died.

When she had at last recovered herself sufficiently to respond to questioning, he asked her what had happened to Edward. She looked round at him, astonished.

"What? You mean you don't know?"

Atherton shook his head.

"I fear not. The Reverend Lethaby sent me a telegram, but it was not specific."

She snorted.

"Lethaby! Much use he's been, and much use he'll be if he should stay on, which I pray God he will not. He didn't tell you what happened to the Reverend Atherton, then?"

Atherton shook his head again.

"Well, it's as much as I might have expected. And you come all this way without knowing what befell your brother!"

"And what did befall him?"

The good lady seemed on the point of bursting into further floods of tears, but with a struggle she composed herself.

"He fell down dead of an apostolic fit, sir."

"That sounds very appropriate," murmured Atherton soothingly, casting me a rueful glance. "And where was he when this dreadful thing happened?"

"Why, in the rectory, sir. It was a very strange affair, as no doubt you'll discover for yourself. There's been talk, Dr Atherton, sir, as you will soon hear. Seems that when Mr Lethaby went to church this morning for matins, he found all the doors locked fast against him, and a great piece of paper on the door of the south porch, with writing on it."

"Writing?" Atherton wrinkled his nose. I could see the thought as though emblazoned on his forehead: surely his brother, of all people, had no pretensions to be a second Luther? "Do you have any idea what it said?"

She shook her head vigorously.

"No, sir, that I don't. I'm not a lettered woman myself, though I know my figures well enough and can tell a 'Paid' from an 'Owing'. But 'tis still there if you want to read it for yourself. And no doubt Mr Lethaby has read and understood it."

"Well, go on – what happened after Lethaby found the doors locked?"

The landlady's hands were busy in her lap, scrunching her apron round and round into a tight ball, then releasing it. I noticed the serving girl's head peep round the door, her eyes huge in a pallid face, then pull away again.

"Seems he – meaning Mr Lethaby, sir – went straight to the rectory and knocked, but had no answer. That was when he grew concerned. Seeing as he had no key, he hurried to Albert Ryman's house, as is the churchwarden, for he knew Albert does keep a spare set of keys for church and rectory both."

"I'm sorry," I interrupted, "but in a parish as small as this, surely the curate must have lived in the rectory himself." I glanced at Atherton. "You did say your brother had neither wife nor children."

He nodded.

"Yes, that would indeed have been a suitable arrangement. But, as I told you, Edward was not of a gregarious temperament. And, to be honest, Lethaby is not an easy man to be with. Edward needed him, for, in spite of appearances, this is quite a wide parish, when you take the outlying farms and some small hamlets into account. However, he resented the idea of sharing his home with another man, and insisted that Lethaby live in a little cottage of his own at the end of the village. The arrangement seemed to suit both of them, although Lethaby has never been happy with his own quarters. Conditions there are rather basic, to say the least."

"I see." I turned back to Mrs O'Reilly. "I do apologise, Mrs O'Reilly. Please go on."

"Well, sir, the Reverend Lethaby and Albert Ryman, they upped and headed back down to the rectory like hares, and let theyselves in. I heard this from Albert's wife herself, otherwise, sir, I'd never have believed a word on it.

"They'd noticed the curtains in the rector's bedroom were still closed, so they reckoned as he might have been took ill in the night, knowing as he were so sickly already. So, upstairs they went and knocked on rector's door, and again no answer.

"'This looks bad,' said Albert, though Mr Lethaby was just stood there all come-over like, and not knowing what to say or do. It was Albert took courage and opened the door, and what he saw, Alice – that's his wife, sir – reckons he won't forget if he lives till he be two hundred."

She paused, partly, I thought, for effect, partly, in all fairness to the good woman, in order to steel her nerves for the description that followed.

"The Reverend Atherton – God save his soul – was kneeling bolt upright in the middle of the floor, and at first Albert thought he were in some sort of trance. But a second look, and it was clear he were stone dead, and a look on his face that would turn milk. A horrid look, as though he'd seen something he oughtn't to have seen, and his eyes as near as popped out of his head."

"That's enough, Mrs O'Reilly," I interrupted. "I'm sure Dr Atherton doesn't want to hear all this."

Atherton placed a hand on my hand and shook his head.

"It's all right, really. Let her go on. I want to know everything."

She glanced at him, then at me. I nodded, and she picked up courage to finish her tale.

"Well, sir, it weren't just the look on Rector's face that gave Albert such a nasty turn. It was –" she lowered her voice, and glanced round the room, as though to make sure no one else was listening – "something heathen, or so Albert reckoned. The rector were kneeling there in a circle of some kind, with candles all round him, dozens of them, some gone out, some still burning. He had his Bible in one hand, and a cross in the other, and a look on his face like he'd seen the devil."

Her hand inadvertently made the sign of the cross over her breast, a gesture, I later learned from Atherton, she had acquired from her Catholic husband. Atherton looked at me, almost with reproach, as though his brother's singular death served as confirmation of what I had so strenuously tried to deny on our first meeting. For myself, I felt only shame that I had not acted sooner, though God alone knows what action I might have taken to prevent such a fearful turn of events.

"The Reverend Lethaby offered to stay behind and take care of the rector. Albert, meanwhile, headed along for March, where he found Dr Sillerton, and brought him back at once. When they came to the rectory, Mr Lethaby had somehow or other managed to lay the rector on his bed. All the candles and whatnot had been cleared from the room, saving for the Bible and the cross. And Lethaby says to Albert he's not to utter a word about any of that to anyone, though he told his wife, as a man ought to, and I had it from her.

"Doctor said it was an apostolic fit that took your dear brother, and no doubt it's a fitting thing in the clergy to go that way when their time comes, though for myself I can't see what's apostolic about seeing the devil."

She paused, sneaking fearful glances right and left again, as though expecting the devil himself to walk into the room.

"The strange thing is," she went on, "that, no sooner had the doctor finished with the rector, than he was called to Mrs Manning's house to see her William. You know who I mean, sir, don't you?"

Atherton nodded and looked at me.

"William Manning was the choirboy who fell ill. You may remember that my brother mentioned him in his notes."

"Yes, indeed. I was meaning to ask if you knew what became of him."

"Well, he fell into a fever, then a coma of some sort, and I understand his life has been feared for ever since." He turned to Mrs O'Reilly. "Don't tell me the boy succumbed as well."

She shook her head, and for the first time a smile appeared on her lips.

"Why, no, sir – quite the opposite. He'd come out of his spell that very night, and was up and eating breakfast, as bright and lively as he'd ever been, thank God. The doctor gave him a looking over and said he could be back at school in a week or so, when he'd got his strength back. It's like a miracle, sir."

"I'm delighted to hear it, truly I am," declared Atherton, and he too smiled. "It has brought some sunshine into what has been one of the darkest days of my life. I pray the boy continues to improve. But where is my brother now, Mrs O'Reilly?"

The landlady looked despondent again.

"He's still in the rectory, sir. Mr Lethaby wanted to lay him out in the church and to set someone there all night to pray over him, but it seems that when Albert went to find the keys of the church, both those belonging to the Reverend Atherton and those he keeps himself were gone."

Atherton looked at her in amazement.

"But who could have taken them?"

"Albert reckons as it was the rector. He'd been with Albert a couple of days before, and he'd been alone in the room where the keys are kept. They've looked all through the rectory, but when I last heard, none had been found."

"My brother evidently wanted to keep people out."

"So it appears," I said. "Look, Atherton, if you don't mind, I'd like very much to see this inscription, if it's still on the church door as you say."

"It is, sir," broke in Mrs O'Reilly. "The Reverend Lethaby wanted to have it took down, but Albert argued with him and said it should stay where it is till someone comes out from the cathedral, for if there's trouble over the matter of the keys, the writing on the paper may be a sort of evidence to show the rector was responsible."

"I heard the bell tolling as we came to the village," I said. "How did they get into the tower if the church is locked?"

"The bell tower's quite separate from the body of the church. That's to say, it has its own entrance. I take it that wasn't locked?"

"No, sir. It was the only door left open, and the key to the bell chamber had been left with Ezra Stukeley, the sexton. He went up this evening to toll the passing bell for your brother, forty-nine rings as I counted."

"Yes, that would be right: a ring for every year of a man's life." He paused, musing. "Forty-nine years," he said. "Not long at all."

30

"No, sir. My husband lived near twenty years above that. It's a grievous thing for a man to be taken in his prime."

A silence followed, filled with rumination on mortality. Atherton shifted on his seat and looked at me.

"Are you up to a walk?" he asked.

I nodded.

"Then let's be off."

Five

It had grown dark outside. Dark, and very cold. Gas had not reached Thornham St Stephen, much less electricity, and the only lights were those that glimmered out, as though by accident, from a couple of half-shuttered windows. Mrs O'Reilly had lent us a lantern, and, while Atherton went a pace or two ahead with it held high, I hobbled behind on my crutches. The road was a bed of frozen mud, but preferable to me as a surface on which to move than the cobbled pavement on either side.

"An apoplectic fit," murmured Atherton as we passed the grocer's shop.

"I'm sorry?"

"That must be what Mrs O'Reilly meant. But what can have angered Edward to such a pitch that he dropped down dead?"

I took a deep breath before answering.

"Perhaps it wasn't anger that provoked the fit, but fear," I said. "From what Mrs O'Reilly told us, I begin to think your brother lived in mortal dread of something, and that he sought to banish it with his candles and crucifix."

"Bell, book, and candle . . . Yes, I think you may be right."

The church loomed up out of the darkness like the shadow of a great ship on an ocean without waves. It seemed no

32

more substantial than that, yet its presence seemed oppressive and cold.

"You do not think my brother suffered?" Atherton asked tentatively. I heard the plea for reassurance in his voice, but, much as I might have wanted to, I could not in all conscience give him false comfort.

"On the contrary, I fear he may have suffered greatly," I said. "I wish it were otherwise, but I think not. Not in body, I do not mean that, but in spirit, very greatly."

"I see. And now – do you think his sufferings are over?"

I could not find the courage to answer. At that moment, we came to the south door, protected from the elements by a large stone porch. Even in the insufficient light that came from the lantern, I could see that the porch was a late addition to an original Norman entrance, the latter adorned with fine carvings.

Atherton raised his lantern, and we saw at once, pinned to the door, a sheet of white paper bearing Edward Atherton's letterhead. On it, in a fine hand, Atherton had written out two quotations from Scripture, separated by a cross, as follows:

This gate shall be shut, it shall not be opened, and no man shall enter in by it.

✝

And he set the porters at the gate of the house of the Lord, that none which was unclean in any thing should enter in.

That was all. No signature, no further inscription of any kind. Just a bare prohibition, and an injunction against uncleanliness. What abomination had Edward Atherton sought to guard against?

"The first is from Ezekiel," I said. "The second is familiar, but I forget its source. First or Second Chronicles, perhaps."

"What can it mean?"

"Well, obviously your brother wanted to keep people out of his church."

"Don't be such a dolt. Of course that's what he was doing. But why? For one thing, he had absolutely no right in canon law."

"Are you quite sure of that?"

"Pretty sure. He would require permission from the rural dean, and very considerable grounds for his decision."

"Such as?"

Atherton shrugged.

"You'd have to ask a churchman, I'm afraid. Perhaps if the sanctity of the church had been compromised in some way." He shivered, looking uneasily round him.

"I don't like it here," he said. "I think we should leave."

I too shivered. It was cold and dark, but something else troubled me, something much less material. Here, at the church door, where I might have expected an odour of sanctity, I sensed only evil.

"I agree," I muttered, and, leaning on Atherton's arm, I hobbled back to the village.

Lethaby was waiting for us in the rectory study, already installed there, as Atherton remarked to me later, as if God Himself had set him down in it. A bright fire roared in the hearth, and I – habitué of the college cellar that I am – detected in the air a faint perfume of fine sherry recently decanted. Lethaby rose languidly, one hand extended towards us, the other held tightly behind his back.

He was a man of medium height, but thin, so that he seemed

taller than he really was. His thinness was that of one who contrives to woo others with a show of asceticism and a general air of self-denial, yet the man impressed me quite otherwise. Our short acquaintance did nothing to dispel my first impression, indeed the better I came to know him, the more certain I grew that Simon Lethaby was cant personified.

"This is Professor Richard Asquith," Atherton said, introducing me. "He has come from Cambridge to lend me moral support."

Lethaby's eyebrows lifted slightly and fell again. I could see his emotionless eyes summing me up.

"Asquith, eh? The author of *An Analytical Description of Dee's Monas Hieroglyphica*, am I not right?"

I answered that he was, and he offered me his hand and a thin smile to go with it.

"A magnificent book," he said, "if a trifle over the head of a mere amateur like myself."

He said this with such an air of superiority that I very nearly recoiled.

"You are familiar with Dee?" I asked. "It seems a curious interest for a cleric."

"I read much in the period," he answered. "It was a time of great crisis for the Church. Queen Elizabeth herself is a fascinating woman." He paused, at a loss to account for my presence, and turned back to Atherton.

"My dear Atherton, I am so distressed that we should meet again under such melancholy circumstances. I believe you feared something of this sort, did you not?"

Atherton ignored the question. I could see there was little affection between the two men.

"I would like to see my brother, if I may. We were told his body is here in the rectory."

Lethaby, shrugging off the rebuff, nodded.

"He is lying upstairs in his bedroom," he said. "Morris, the undertaker from March, came this afternoon to lay him out. A good man, Morris. Very respectful. I would not have left him here, but, as you know, the keys to the church have been mislaid."

"Has the doctor certified the cause of death?"

"But of course. There will be no need for a post-mortem. A heart seizure brought on by apoplexy, that is all."

"And you have no idea what caused this apoplexy?"

Lethaby shook his head. He was making a conscious effort to appear at ease, but I could tell that, underneath, he was anything but.

"None at all."

"He had not quarrelled with anyone?"

"Good heavens, no. Your brother was a most peaceable man, as you know."

"Nevertheless, even a peaceable man may be drawn into a argument."

"To my knowledge, nothing like that occurred. I was with him last night until almost ten o'clock. We dined together, then went over the parish accounts. There was nothing unusual in them, nothing that might have alarmed Edward. We said good-night, and, as far as I know, he intended to go straight to bed."

Atherton was growing agitated.

"What I wish to know is what took place after that. I have heard that my brother was found under . . . peculiar circumstances."

"My dear Atherton!" Lethaby looked shocked and pained, yet I could see a flicker of annoyance in his eyes.

Atherton went on to relate what Mrs O'Reilly had told

him. As he did so, Lethaby's annoyance grew and took full possession of him. Alongside it, I detected not a little anxiety.

"Why, this is all quite absurd. It's the most absurd thing I have ever heard. I shall have words with Mrs O'Reilly. What can she be thinking of to fabricate such a nonsensical story?"

"You deny it, then?"

"Good heavens, of course I do. Your brother was found dead in his own bed. Whatever the exact cause of his demise, I assure you there was nothing untoward about it."

"I'm relieved to hear it," said Atherton, though his voice lacked conviction. He sighed and rose to his feet.

"I would like to go up now," he said. "You don't have to accompany me, I know the way." He turned to me. "Asquith, do you think you can climb the stairs?"

I had avoided stairs as much as possible in the past few weeks, but when necessary I could manage them.

"One at a time," I said. "You'll have to give me a hand."

Lethaby offered to accompany us, but Atherton insisted he stay downstairs. He was polite, but firm, and Lethaby knew he was overruled.

"Good Lord," said Atherton in a low voice, as we started up the stairs. "That man is the greatest hypocrite on God's earth. He used to infuriate my brother terribly."

"Yes, he does appear self-serving. I wonder your brother tolerated him at all."

"Oh, Lethaby has friends at court. To be precise, the Dean of Ely is his uncle. He has expectations of higher things than Thornham St Stephen."

"I wonder he came to be here at all."

Atherton gave a dry laugh.

"Mr Lethaby does nothing by accident. It is precisely

to deflect accusations of nepotism that he seeks no major preferment now, but plays the country curate, a man of humble means and humble ambitions. But take my word for it, he will not remain a curate long. My brother's death will have been a most welcome boost to his prospects. He can confidently expect the rectorship, and can afford to spend a year or two here before moving elsewhere. He is still only seven and twenty."

I climbed each step as though it were a small hill, first raising my good leg to the step above, then pulling myself up with the help of the banister. Atherton held an oil-lamp to light my way. The stairway was dark. I felt a growing sense of apprehension as we mounted the stairs. The feeling I had experienced in the church porch was returning, less acute, yet unmistakable.

With each flicker of the light against the wall, I expected . . . Well, I confess I did not know quite what to expect, only that something was here and that the unfortunate Atherton's death had not expelled it. I still knew next to nothing about the business, but the deeper I went in, the more worried I grew that I was passing beyond my depth.

The Reverend Atherton's room was the second on the right off the first landing. My companion opened the door slowly, and I noticed that his hand trembled slightly as he turned the knob. Until now, he had seemed to me very well composed, and I had thought that, knowing less than I of these matters, his mind was less disturbed than mine. I realised that I had never talked with him about his beliefs. It could not be assumed that, since his brother had been a rector, he himself was a believer.

Lighted candles had been placed by the head of the corpse, one on either side. The dead man lay on top of the covers, dressed in the black garb of an old-fashioned cleric, complete with gaiters. In spite of the best efforts of the undertaker, his face still exhibited signs of the horror that been imprinted on it when he was found. I watched as Atherton approached the bed and knelt down beside it. He remained there, silent and alone, though whether he was praying for his brother's soul or just lost in his own thoughts, I could not tell.

While he knelt, my eyes roamed about the bedchamber. There were no overt signs of anything amiss. It was a well-found room of generous size, well proportioned, and furnished in a style appropriate to a churchman of Atherton's inclinations. There was nothing lavish or extravagant, no hint of luxury or self-indulgence; but the whole effect was pleasing to the senses, for the furniture and fittings were of the highest quality, and it was evident that both taste and independent means had gone into their choice.

On one wall hung a drawing – by Butterfield, if I am not mistaken – of All Saints, Margaret Street, the paragon of the Gothic revivalists. Beside it had been placed a reproduction of a medieval painting, which I recognised as the crucifixion from the Abingdon Missal. Other prints and etchings covered each of the four walls.

I returned my gaze to the bed, and to the body of Edward Atherton. His lips were parted in a dreadful rictus, the whole face portraying an expression of utter terror, as though, even in death, he could see what he had most feared in life. Clasped between his folded hands was a large Bible. I wondered if it could be the same one his brother had mentioned.

Atherton sighed deeply, then eased himself to his feet.

"I'm sorry to leave you standing there, Richard," he said. "I just wanted to take leave of Edward. Mother arrives tomorrow, and then the rest of the family will descend. This was my only chance."

"Would you not prefer it if I left you alone with him for a while?"

He looked at me, troubled, then shook his head firmly.

"No, indeed. I don't think I could stay in here for a moment on my own. It's bad enough as it is. These shadows make my flesh creep."

I nodded. The room was hardly conducive to peace of mind. There was an oppressive air of religious melancholy everywhere.

"Is that your brother's Bible?" I asked, pointing to the volume that lay on the corpse's breast.

Atherton looked at it carefully and nodded.

"I hesitate to suggest such a thing, but in view of the confusion there may be here tomorrow . . ." I looked earnestly at him. "I would very much like to see the papers you say he had in it."

Atherton nodded.

"Yes, I think you're right. It's too late to help him now, but perhaps it may save some other poor devil's life."

He walked over to a bookcase on the other side of the room, and returned carrying another Bible, a little smaller than the one we meant to remove, but, like it, bound in black leather. Taking a deep breath, he reached for the Bible that lay between his brother's hands, but at the last moment drew back.

"I'm sorry," he whispered, "but I'm afraid I can't bear to touch him."

I did it for him, exchanging the Bibles without disturbing the body. As I did so, the first Bible, the one into which Edward Atherton had slipped his little pieces of paper, fell open in my hand, as though to a spot at which it had often been turned.

I saw it had fallen open in the Book of Ezekiel. Atherton had defaced both pages, blacking out every line with ink,

40

scoring the paper hard enough at times to tear small holes in its surface.

No, I was mistaken, the writing had not been completely blacked out. A single verse remained. I held the book to the light and read.

Evigilavit adversum te, the text ran, *ecce venit.* It watcheth for thee; behold, it is come.

I shut the book and said nothing, but my hands were shaking.

Six

Lethaby was waiting for us downstairs. He seemed slightly anxious, as though he had been expecting us to return furnished with complaints about the manner in which Edward Atherton had been laid out.

"I am so sorry," he said, "that things are not as they should be. The whole thing has been so sudden, and this business of the church keys . . ." He paused. "You have heard of their disappearance?"

We nodded.

"Yes, well, this business of the vanishing keys has put us out terribly. I would have preferred your brother to pass the night in the church, before the altar, but it was impossible to gain admittance without damaging the doors. The nearest locksmith is a man called Dunn from Wisbech. He was away on business all day, but his wife has promised to send him here first thing in the morning. Once the church is reopened, your brother may be moved there for a village service prior to his removal to Ely."

"Ely? Why should he be taken there?" Atherton seemed shocked.

"Surely you knew that your brother is to be laid to rest beside your father in the cathedral. I understand the dean means to attend, and perhaps even the bishop himself – I have taken it upon my own shoulders to write to them, and to other members of the chapter. Your brother –" he inclined his head to Atherton with a most oleaginous smile – "was greatly loved by his fellow clergy.

"Of course," he looked grave for a moment, as though to elicit our sympathy "you will understand that . . . should any rumours concerning your brother's demise reach the ears of the dean . . . I think I need not say what an unfortunate impression that might make. And your dear mother would, of course, be so distressed, especially if there were to be any question about the propriety of a cathedral burial."

"You don't need to spell it out, Lethaby," said Atherton. "By all means have your bishop, your dean, and a flock of canons major and minor, since it pleases you and will no doubt please my mother. But I would prefer to talk more about this tomorrow. Professor Asquith and I have had a long journey. We will dine at the Three Windmills and have an early night. No doubt we shall see you in the morning."

He paused as though a troubling thought had occurred to him.

"Do you mean to spend the night here?"

For the first time Lethaby's composure seemed to crack. He licked his lips, and I could not but notice the small motion he made as he glanced at the ceiling, in the direction of the room in which his rector lay.

"I . . . regret . . . that is to say, I am invited to dine this evening with Sir Philip at the manor house. He is sending a carriage for me. Since Kennett House is some distance, he has suggested that I stay over. I did, of course, mention that you were to be here, but I felt that—" he flashed his most winning smile – "under the circumstances of such a recent bereavement, you would not wish to be in company.

Sir Philip quite understood. He sends his condolences, of course." He paused, as though uncertain how best to end this sorry narration. "Naturally," he went on hurriedly, having spied the gap in his defences, "I would not go myself were it not that Sir Philip and I have urgent business to discuss, business that cannot be put off."

I saw Atherton suppress his rage. Later, he told me that Sir Philip Ousby, the local landowner, provided the benefices for the parishes of Thornham St Stephen, Thornham St Paul, and the remoter Thornham-Cum-Quy. Clearly Lethaby did not intend to lose a moment in winning the good Sir Philip to his cause.

Atherton and I returned to the inn much fallen in spirits. It is never a cheering thing to be in the company of the dead, but the circumstances of Edward Atherton's death and the happenings, as yet but dimly perceived, that had led up to it could not fail but to leave even the most buoyant spirit downcast. More than that, I felt a very real sensation of imminent dread, though I had then but the vaguest notion of what inspired it.

Mrs O'Reilly prepared a splendid meal for us – finer, I have no doubt, than anything served that night to the Reverend Lethaby. The late Mr O'Reilly had left behind a recipe for Irish stew, and his widow brought it to the table along with a most delightful dish known as champ, another of her husband's Irish delicacies – potatoes mashed and prepared with spring onions, milk, and butter. To the stew itself she had added dumplings from a recipe of her own, together with generous portions of the best local ale, and large glasses of the same brew to wash it down. We had neither of us felt much appetite, yet our plates were wiped clean and our glasses emptied as though we had been walkers come in from a long hike.

We lingered over the meal and the whiskies that followed,

talking quietly, staring into the flame-filled hearth of the little private room that had been put aside for us. From time to time, the voices of the inn's other customers broke through the walls, the subdued tones of men from a small community that has known recent death. No doubt Mrs O'Reilly would have made sure they knew that the Reverend Atherton's brother was her guest, and with him a professor from Cambridge, a place they had often heard of but never visited.

No doubt, too, she was doing her best to spread Alice Ryman's tale of the discovery of the rector's body. I had spoken with her briefly, and tried to dissuade her from giving wider circulation to the rumour; but I knew it was probably the most exciting thing that had happened in Thornham St Stephen in the last hundred years, and had no great hopes that her natural volubility would not burst through somehow.

Instinctively, both Atherton and I steered off that subject ourselves. I knew I should have to return to it in time, with or without him, for something in Thornham St Stephen was amiss, and I knew that what had been so carelessly awakened would not return to rest without great trouble. But that night I preferred to stick to less disturbing matters – mutual friends, academic topics, the recent gossip surrounding the Master of Pembroke, the declining quality of undergraduates.

It was late when we took ourselves to bed. We had a room each, at either end of a short, unfurnished corridor. Upstairs, the inn, that had been so full of cheer below, was cold and draughty, and dismal in appearance. We said good-night to one another, and arranged to meet the following morning for an early breakfast.

My room gave an impression of having been slept in very little. No doubt overnight guests were a rarity in such a remote part of the fens. The furnishings reflected this disuse, being mean bits and pieces that had been shoved into the room for want of anywhere else to store them. The thin curtains that covered the window did nothing to keep the cold out, nor did the pitiful fire that burned in the hearth make serious inroads on the damp chill that pervaded the air.

The bed, at least, was warm. Mrs O'Reilly had taken care to place two warming-pans in it, one at the top and one at the bottom. I removed them and put them to one side, then slid between the sheets, grateful for all the Mrs O'Reillys of the world, and mine above all. Smiling, I turned down the lamp, though I did not extinguish it altogether.

I was exhausted, and my body was warm and comfortable – inevitable preconditions for sleep, or so I imagined. Yet minute after minute passed, and sleep would not come. The harder I tried, the more elusive it became. In the near-darkness, my thoughts kept returning to that silent figure in the rectory bedroom, and to the words he had left in his mutilated Bible. When half an hour or more had passed, I was twisting and turning, unable to find repose. My leg had started to pain me, adding its twinges to my mental torments.

In the end, I gave in and turned the light up full again. I felt hot, unpleasantly so, in spite of the cold outside. With an effort, I struggled out of bed. My dressing-gown was hanging at its foot, and I put it on. By now, the fire had burned very low indeed, but there were some coals remaining in the scuttle; I hobbled over and tossed them on, and in about ten minutes bright flames lit up the room.

If I could not sleep, I might at least read. I had brought one or two books with me: the first volume of Odericus Vitalis's *Historia Ecclesiastica*, in the edition of le Prévost and Delisle, and Riley's edition of Thomas Walsingham's *Historia Anglicana*. Taking them from my bag, I leafed through one and then the other, but found myself unable to summon up the necessary concentration to read more than a few lines. My thoughts were elsewhere, and not easily to be distracted.

Edward Atherton's Bible was on my bedside table, where I had left it, not meaning to look at it or its contents again until the morning. I took all the slips of paper from it and brought them to the fire, where I began carefully to go through them, placing them, as well as I could, in chronological order. When I had the sheets laid out, I began to read. This time my concentration did not fail me.

Seven

Cowper approached me today after evensong. He says his men are grumbling, and that they refuse to touch the de Lindesey tomb. I told him I would not tolerate such interference in my work, and asked what possible reason the men could have. His answer was that there are local legends concerning the tomb, and that it is widely believed it should never be disturbed. I showed him the archdeacon's certificate which permits the work to be carried out, and gave him the benefit of a discourse on the idle fancies of the lower classes, reminded him just how much work – and money – he stood to lose, and ordered him to start first thing tomorrow.

Work began on the tomb today, and almost as soon ended. I heartily wish I had never come here, or purposed to restore this place. Cowper's men were right: the de Lindesey tomb ought never to have been disturbed.

I went to church early to meet Cowper and his labourers on their arrival, thinking to give them what moral support they might require. The men's faces were sullen, and I could tell they had turned up on sufferance; but Cowper chivvied them, and I think my presence – I still wore my cassock –

48

reassured them. There were four of them, all local men, one or two of them regular churchgoers whom I knew by sight, if not by name.

Some time was spent examining the various cracks that had appeared in the side of the monument. Cowper pointed them out to me one at a time, showing how the uneven pressure exerted by the upper section made it impossible to effect a proper repair. There had been earlier attempts to seal up the cracks, but none of them had held for very long, and in the end the attempt had been abandoned. The top would have to be winched off, then each of the side pieces repaired and reset.

'Can you do all this without disturbing the remains?' I asked. Cowper said that they would do their best, but that much would depend on what they found once the tomb was opened. I gave him permission to go ahead, and they brought in some heavy equipment from outside and set to work.

It took above an hour to set up the winch, a great wooden monstrosity which Cowper had hired from a construction firm in Peterborough. While two of the men worked at this under Cowper's supervision, the others busied themselves in loosening the mortar that divided one half of the superstructure from the other, and the upper stone (the portion that bears the effigy of de Lindesey) from the lower.

By the time all this was ready, it was past lunch time. The men had worked continually all morning, with scarcely a break. I thanked them for all they had done so far, and headed off to the rectory for my own lunch.

When I returned, I found that they had been waiting for me before resuming work. I could see the apprehension on their faces, as though they were about to summon up the devil himself.

' ''Tis all right, is it, Rector, what we're about to do?' asked one of the men, Ezekiel Finch. 'Only, openin' a grave, it seems like . . . well, like sakerlidge.'

I smiled and put my hand on his shoulder. It is the sort of gesture, I have found, that means much to the working classes, and it seemed to put Finch at ease.

'It would only be sacrilege if we were to remove the bones entirely, or put them to profane use. Since it is our intention to rebury them within the chancel, and since I shall perform the service of reburial myself, you may rest assured that nothing will be done here that is not approved of by the Church.'

Finch thanked me, and they set to work. I watched from a little distance, by the rood screen. A feather chisel was used to raise one edge of the right-hand slab until two flat hooks could be inserted. Trestles and boards had been set up on one side, ready to receive the lid as it came across.

The men pulled on a single rope, and the chains fastened to the tomb took the strain, raising the top section far enough to allow Finch to slip a roller underneath. I watched with my heart in my mouth, for I knew that if any part of the apparatus slipped or gave way the monument could fall and be irreparably ruined.

The winch was secured, and the men now took up positions at either end of the tomb lid, in order to push it over the roller onto the trestles. It was hard work, for they had to keep the whole thing balanced as it moved. Cowper kept a close eye on them. Two men pushed from the tomb end, while two brought the slab onto rollers laid on the table.

It had travelled no more than six inches when something dreadful happened. I am still not sure how it came about. All seemed to be going well, when I suddenly became aware of . . . I am not sure how best to describe it, but it seemed to be

50

a darkening about the tomb. I thought I saw . . . a shadow rise from the aperture. The others saw it too, and one man, Cobbitt, screamed and fell to the ground as if attacked, clutching his throat. The chain holding the slab at his end was dislodged, and the entire lid went off balance, slipping on the roller and falling forward, in spite of the efforts of Cobbitt's mate to hold it firm.

The full weight of the slab struck the trestles, unbalancing them, and in less than a second it crashed to the ground, catching poor Finch by the leg and pinning him underneath.

I ran across to help, and as I did so the first thing that struck me was a dreadful stench that seemed to come from the tomb. It occurred to me then, and occurs to me again now, that this frightful odour may have been the cause of Cobbitt's falling back.

Finch was on his back, in terrible pain, his right leg twisted dreadfully, his face as white as marble. I did my best to comfort him, while the others slaved to fix the winch to the slab and haul it up far enough to free the poor man's leg. I remained bent over him, praying for all I was worth. It seemed to take hours, though I think it may have been at the most ten minutes. Finch lost consciousness not long after I joined him. The floor was wet with blood, and I knew there could be no saving his leg.

In the end, the lid of the tomb moved sufficiently to let Cowper move Finch out. His leg had been all but severed just below the knee, and he was still losing blood freely.

It was then, just as we extricated him, that I heard something to chill my blood. Dry laughter that seemed to come from somewhere near the reredos. None of the others seemed to notice it, and I said nothing, not wishing to frighten them any more than they were already. Tonight, as I sit writing this, I

wonder if I can have been mistaken, disturbed as I was by the
accident and the sight of that unfortunate man's leg. And yet,
it did sound terribly real. Indeed, I can still hear it, as though
it continues, barely audible, beneath my own rafters.

I laid the papers down on the floor beside me, and looked up,
blinking and staring blindly, into the fire. In my mind's eye,
I could see it all re-enacted – the movement of a shadow, the
man's cry, the crashing slab, the other man pinned by a dead
man's effigy.

I sat like that for a long time, not wishing to read any further,
watching the flames burn lower and lower, the coals whiten and
turn to vivid ash, the ashes lose their luminosity and grow cold
in the dead hearth.

Shivering, I got up and went to the window. I needed to look
outside, to see anything but the little room in which I sat. In
any case, I had no desire to return to bed, and even less to turn
down my lamp and shut my eyes in a vain attempt to sleep. I
had heard of a case like this one, not many years previously,
in France, and I knew that it had turned out badly.

The sky was overlaid by thin, scudding clouds, whipped
rapidly past by a wind out of the Wash. Now and then, a gap
would reveal a three-quarter moon, corpse-white and remote
and on the wane.

I could see the church tower and the west front from where
I stood. It rose up, dark and somehow menacing, while the
coming and going of the moonlight cast peculiar shadows
across its stone walls.

As I watched, the moon emerged into a long patch of clear
sky, illuminating the entire west wall. Something caught my
eye, high up on the tower, and, as I strained to see more clearly,
a shadow detached itself from the stone and began to climb

deliberately downwards, pausing, hovering, then moving off again. And then another mass of clouds rushed across the moon, and I could see no more. When the next stretch of moonlight came, the shadow had gone. Perhaps, I thought, it had never been there at all.

I crossed to the bedside table and looked at my pocket watch. It was after one o'clock. I sighed. The thought of dressing and going out again on such a night was deeply repellent. But I had no choice. What I had to do, had to be done that night.

Eight

I knocked gently on Atherton's door. He too must have been wide awake, for he answered in a matter of moments. His hair was dishevelled, and his eyes were red, and I knew that grief had kept him from his sleep as surely as fear had kept me from mine.

"What's wrong?" he asked. He pulled his dressing-gown around him, shivering in the cold from the corridor. "Why are you dressed? Is anything wrong?"

"I think we should go to the rectory," I said.

He looked at me in astonishment.

"At this time in the morning? What on earth for?"

"I can't explain, there isn't time. I'd go alone, but I can't do it with this wretched leg. Will you come with me?"

Now that the idea was sinking in, I could see him grow reluctant. I confess it had little appeal to me either, and freely admit that it was not just my leg which made me desirous of company.

"Can't it wait until daylight, at least?" he asked.

I shook my head.

"It is important," I said, "or I would not have come to you."

He hesitated a moment longer, then nodded.

"Wait for me there," he said. "I'll get dressed."

*   *   *

The door of the inn had not been locked – burglars are not a common menace in the countryside – and Atherton and I were able to sneak out unobserved. It was very cold indeed now, and our breath hung all around us, as though sculpted by the light of our lantern.

Thornham St Stephen was utterly still. It was as if the deep notes of the passing bell had cast its inhabitants into an everlasting sleep. Nothing moved or breathed. There were no lights anywhere, and no sounds, not even a dog barking or a wild creature crying in the fields. I was cold and sick at heart. Each time the moon came scuttling from behind the clouds, I started at shadows like a child. Atherton, pacing ahead of me, saw none of this; but he had caught my mood and was, I sensed, as ill at ease as I.

The moon disappeared behind more clouds as we came to the door of the rectory. From what little I had seen, it was a dismal building, built some time in the earliest part of this century and, judging by the rooms I had seen earlier, subsequently inhabited by a succession of cheeseparing clerics and their embittered wives. What, after all, is a fine church to life in the wilderness? The very mortar of the place was riddled with disappointment and frustration. I could feel them seeping through the walls like damp.

As I had expected, Lethaby, a city-dweller at heart, had locked the door and driven off to dinner with the key in his trouser pocket. Fortunately, the rectory was set back a little from the village proper, in its own garden, which meant that Atherton and I were able to make our way unobserved to the rear. Here, looking up, I saw the great dark bulk of the church looming above us. I looked away again, fearful of what the moon might show me if it came clear of the clouds once more.

A sash window had been left open. Passing the lamp to me, Atherton pulled it up and scrambled through the aperture. I handed the lamp back to him, and he opened the back door to let me in.

As I limped over the threshold, I felt it at once – something was already in the house, something old and cunning and full of malice. I had no way of knowing whether or not it was aware of our presence as I was aware of it. But I had to assume the worst.

"What's wrong?" whispered Atherton.

"Shhh," I hissed, holding up one hand. "Can't you feel it?"

He stood very still for a while, then looked at me. His cheeks had turned pale.

"I don't like it," he said. "There's something . . ." He paused. "Something that shouldn't be here."

"You don't have to stay," I told him. "All I needed was help this far. If you'd rather leave, I'll understand. You aren't accustomed to this sort of thing. You could get in my way."

I saw him hesitate. The feeling of malice in the house was strong, and growing stronger by the minute. I felt the hairs on my body rise, and a voice inside my head urged me repeatedly to run. Atherton too seemed to ponder flight, but after brief deliberation, shook his head.

"No," he declared, "I'd prefer to stay here, if you don't mind. If there is any danger, I have no right to leave you to face it alone."

"Thank you," I said. "I'd be grateful for your company." I paused, all too conscious of the dark, empty house all around us. "Now," I said, "I think we should make our way upstairs."

His face crumbled.

"Must we go up there? My brother . . ." His voice tailed away.

I knew what he was thinking. I too could imagine his brother, laid out as though waiting for us.

"It's what I came for," I answered.

We made our way into the hall. Heavy ecclesiastical engravings hung on the walls. A stuffed owl stared down at us, its eyes bright in the lamplight. Near it hung a portrait of a stern-faced man dressed in the robes of an Anglican bishop.

"Our father," whispered Atherton, seeing me stare at it. "It was painted by Buckner a few years before Father's death."

"He seems a little stiff and formal."

"Bishops are. Edward would have been one if he'd lived. He had all the needful qualities."

I could almost feel the eyes of the old bishop on us as I began to climb the stairs behind Atherton. Like burglars, we moved in silence, as though we feared to disturb the house's sleeping inhabitants; but the only sleeper here was Edward Atherton, and he would not wake easily.

We had gone about halfway when I became aware of a sound. Atherton heard it too. We both stopped, holding our breaths, and listening hard. It was not long before the sound was repeated, louder this time, a dull moaning sound as of someone in pain or dread. I looked up the dark staircase, in the direction from which the sound had come, and felt myself go cold.

"It has started," I whispered.

"You knew this would happen?"

"Not this exactly. I'm still not sure what's going on. But something like this, yes." I paused, gathering my courage for what inevitably lay ahead. "We must hurry. There's no time to lose."

We made what haste we could, Atherton going ahead, but never too far from me. The moaning grew in frequency and volume, and, as we turned the corner at the top of the stairs, it was clear that it came from Edward Atherton's bedroom.

At the door, we hesitated. Unmistakable sounds of pain came from inside, and neither of us had the courage to open the door, not knowing what we might see once we entered.

"Dear God," whispered Atherton. "What is it?"

"I dare not think," I said. I looked hard at him. "We have to go in. Now more than ever. Are you game?"

By way of answer, he put his hand to the doorknob and turned it hard.

The room was pitch dark. Lethaby had closed the shutters and drawn the curtains, blocking out all external illumination. As we entered, Atherton raised the lamp. His trembling hand caused it to shake, sending ripples of unsteady light across the darkness, confusing my eyes with a host of moving shadows.

"Let me have the lamp," I said.

He passed it to me. My hand was steadier than his, but barely so. I stepped in front of him and thrust the lamp forward.

Edward Atherton's body was still lying on the bed where we had left him. For a few seconds, I thought nothing was amiss, that, after all, I had been mistaken. But as I took another step forward, I saw that his eyes were wide open. The wailing sound we had heard from below was issuing from his parted lips.

"He's alive!" shouted Atherton. "Good God, my brother is still alive."

He was about to dash towards the bed, when I grabbed his arm hard and held him fast.

"For God's sake, man," I pleaded. "That thing is not alive. Don't you understand? That is not your brother on the bed."

"But he's crying out . . ."

"It's not your brother," I repeated, "not any more."

"Surely there's something we can do all the same."

I thought quickly. Not in all my years of investigations had I encountered anything like this before. I could only guess at what was really happening. On the bed, the thing that had been Edward Atherton lay watching and listening.

"Listen," I said, "your brother was a conservative. He may even have had Roman leanings. Do you know if he ever kept consecrated host here or in the church?"

"Yes, yes, I remember – downstairs in the study. He had a small box, a silver box."

"That will be it. Go down quickly and fetch it."

"What about you?"

"I'll be all right. Just go."

He hesitated, then dashing to the bedside, grabbed a candle, which he lit from the lamp.

"Here," he said. "I can't leave you here in the dark."

I took the candle, and he dashed through the door. Moments later, I heard his feet on the stairs. On the bed, the body remained still. Still, but not silent. It had begun to speak, in a stilted, awkward fashion, as though the throat and tongue and lips it used were things unfamiliar to it. The words – if words they were – were unrecognisable, as though it spoke in an alien language. And yet, somewhere in it all I could discern the rudiments of human speech.

The candle flickered in my hand. My leg hurt abominably, and I knew that whatever happened I could not run. All round me shadows moved like small, frightened animals, and the thing on the bed went on babbling. I forced myself to face it.

"Who are you?" I asked. "What do you want here?" I did not even know if it could understand me, but I felt its eyes fasten on me. The hands fluttered momentarily, then grew still. The lips continued to move, spewing out words, whole sentences I could not understand, and as the thing grew in mastery, so the words grew more distinct, though no more comprehensible to me.

"What is your name?" I asked again. It was bitterly cold in that room, and I shivered uncontrollably. All the time, I listened desperately for the sound of Atherton returning.

Suddenly, the thing grew silent. Foam lay on the corners of its mouth. Animated though it was, it had not lost that waxen pallor of absolute death that lay on the skin of face and hands. It was silent, but I knew it kept cold watch on me. I opened my mouth to speak again, but before I could do so, it addressed me, and this time I understood.

"Guillielmus sum. Pro qua disfidete me?" The speech was soft, almost silken, but overlaid with a tone of arrogance or superciliousness that took my breath away.

I stared speechlessly at the thing on the bed. It had spoken in clear Latin, or, if I am to be precise, Church Latin of the Middle Ages. "I am William," it had said. "Why do you defy me?"

It is hard to explain in simple words the impact of that declaration and the demand that followed it; nor am I able to give a lucid description of the emotions I felt on hearing words uttered in a language I had only ever seen before written on the pages of long-forgotten manuscripts. The eyes blazed at me, mocking my horror and my silence. I had to struggle to dredge up the right Latin words with which to formulate an adequate response.

"Go back whence you came. You are not wanted here."

I was answered by a long laugh that faded slowly into silence.

"You have no right here. You have no authority to command me."

"If you will not be commanded, then you must be forced."

The laugh again, from deep in the throat, less mocking than before, touched with the beginnings of triumph. I saw a hand move, slowly, but with growing strength. Soon it would have command of all the limbs. I went to the door and called out, "Atherton! Hurry, man, hurry! You must come now or all is lost."

And, suddenly, Atherton's feet on the stairs, and the shaking of the light as he hurried up, bounding from step to step. He reached the bedroom door and thrust a small box of engraved silver into my hands. I lifted the lid. Inside lay about two dozen wafers, each stamped with the cross.

I turned to face the bed. As the thing caught sight of the wafer, its expression altered.

"Out! Thou nart a prest," it said, and I realised it had switched from Latin to Middle English. *"Thou hast noon auctoritee over me."*

Ignoring this, I stepped towards the bed.

"Help me," I appealed to Atherton. "It may try to fight against us."

To his very great credit, Atherton did not protest. He came forward and held down his brother's body, growing as it was now in strength, and vehement against our interference. While he did so, I forced the lips open and laid the wafer on the corpse's tongue. It tossed its head from side to side, crying aloud, but it could not spit out the offending substance. Suddenly, the body went rigid, and a great trembling followed, passing through every limb and muscle.

"Hold fast," I said. I did not know the words of the Latin exorcism, but I had by heart the Lord's Prayer, and so recited it in a loud voice, over the sound of cries and protests. *Pater noster . . .*

*   *   *

It seemed to take an eternity, but at last I came to the 'Amen', which word I uttered in unison with Atherton. By then the crying and shouting had stopped.

A dense silence followed, a silence full of other silences, so deep and so prolonged it seemed the night must pass before it ended. We stood bent over Edward Atherton's reclaimed body, and at every moment I feared the return of what I had banished. But there was neither sound nor motion, and, in the end, I stepped back from the bed and looked down at the corpse, cold and unmoving as I had first seen it.

"Thank God," whispered Atherton. "Thank God it's all over."

I looked at him. His face was ashen, and his sunken eyes betrayed a weariness and dread that had not been in him before. Perhaps I should have said nothing, perhaps I should have left him with his illusions, for a time at least. But I was tired too, and cold.

"Over?" I said. I shook my head. "On the contrary, it has just begun."

Nine

The next day dawned, grey and dismal, as a cold wind swept across the fens, bringing rain in its wake. Neither Atherton nor I had closed our eyes for the remainder of that night. We had stayed up together in his room, feeding the fire with coals from downstairs, talking of what we had just witnessed. I think he wanted to confront a reality that contradicted all he knew and had experienced.

For my part, it was something of a relief to lay before him what I could of my own experience and knowledge, for I have had long acquaintance with matters of this kind. I told him of other hauntings I had seen, of visitations from beyond the grave, and the descent of evil into the world.

"I will know more," I said, "when I have had time to study your brother's church. I mean to take a close look at the tomb he had opened. It's my firm conviction that it will prove to be the source of whatever evil there is in this place. Only when I know with greater certainty what lies behind it all can I take action to lay it to rest for good."

"But surely, what took place tonight—"

I shook my head.

"That was only a temporary measure. The visitant was right: I am not a priest, and I had no authority over him. All I've done is hold him off for a while."

*   *   *

The service was set to begin at ten. At eight, Atherton and I ventured out, in time to see the locksmith open the south door of the church. The paper pinned there by Atherton's brother had been removed. Lethaby let us in, oblivious of our mood. He seemed smug and well pleased with his dinner the night before.

"Sir Philip sends his very best regards, and his condolences. You must dine with him on a more auspicious occasion, he is most emphatic on that point. You, my dear Professor Asquith, will find him congenial. He is something of an amateur historian. Indeed, he has published a pamphlet on the history of his family which I am sure you will find most interesting. Permit me to give you a copy before you leave."

He then dropped me as smoothly as any politician, and turned to Atherton, saying he must discuss with him the details of the service that was to follow. While Atherton meekly followed the curate into the nave, I slipped outside in order to get my bearings.

Under happier circumstances, I should have enjoyed immensely my first acquaintance with St Stephen's. It is one of our finest parish churches, whose glories have been in no way diminished by the obscurity into which it has so undeservedly fallen. If ever I find the leisure, I shall one day compose a monograph on it, in the hope that it may, in time, take its rightful place among the great English churches. Or, perhaps not: I should not like it to fall into the hands of assorted ecclesiologists, local historians, and tourists, all intent on making it something it is not. And there are, besides, graver considerations that hold me back from ever publicising Thornham St Stephen and its church too widely.

Of the church's history and features, I shall set down here only as much as may shed light on what passed there, or provide the reader with a more vivid image of the place in which so many of these events took place. St Stephen's began life as a dower church of the Benedictine Abbey at Thornham, now sadly fallen into ruin. The church had been granted to the abbey by Sir Roger FitzJocelin, an eleventh-century benefactor, and had remained in its ownership until the dissolution.

The original abbey having been destroyed by the Danes in 864, it was refounded by the Benedictines some one hundred years later. It was a little after the Norman invasion that Sir Roger undertook to expand the abbey and its revenues. Not long after that, a group of monks travelled several miles east of the original foundation to set up a small priory next to the Anglo-Saxon church of St Stephen, whose foundation stone is said to have been laid by St Felix not long after he founded his cathedral at Soham.

But for a stone coffin lid, nothing now remains of that original church now, and precious little of the eleventh-century abbey church. I believe the small crypt contains walls from that period, and there is a stone font next the galilee that shows signs of an early Norman hand; but St Stephen's is essentially a late Norman building that evolves rapidly into Early English and is overlaid at last by the very best of the Perpendicular. With the Dissolution, the buildings of the little monastery were demolished, and their stones removed for the building of Kennett House. But the church, by now the centre of a thriving parish, did not suffer the fate of the mother foundation at Thornham, and in time it passed unscathed through Cromwell's depredations to emerge as an almost intact example of a pre-Reformation English church.

Coming upon it with so little preparation in the greyness of that flat funeral morning, I stood for a long time staring from a distance, as though lost out among the softly moulded graves of

65

the churchyard. An old man, white-bearded and stooped, stood watching from a distance, the only villager in sight.

I glanced up at the church tower, shuddering as I thought of the shadow I had seen on the previous evening. It is an octagonal structure, typical of the region, a turreted Perpendicular shaft soaring high above a circular base to just over one hundred feet – a dizzying height for anyone to climb, even in the most clement of conditions.

The west door had been opened, and I made my way into the church through it, conscious as always of the ambivalence of my feelings. An unbeliever, I am not awed by any sense of the numinous, and yet I am not altogether immune to the air of sanctity and consecrated antiquity common to the very best of churches. It is something I can't explain, a sort of gap in my mental apparatus, an interstice between mind and feeling. Reason and intellect tell me there is no God, that salvation is a fancy, that heaven and hell are peopled by imagination, that the sacraments are rituals for human comfort, nothing more. And yet I know there is damnation for the living, I have seen evil in more than human weakness, I am sensible that not everything may be explained by what we know of the material.

My sensations on entering St Stephen's were, at first, little different from those I had experienced in a hundred other churches, complicated emotions wakened by a mixture of things visual, things audible, and things olfactory – light falling dimly through high lancet windows in a tall clerestory, stone mellowed by the warm breath of generations, lozenges of colour on a marbled floor, the scent of incense, the odours of candle-wax and smoke, and, above everything, that most profound of silences, that very essence of hushed wakefulness that is to be found only in sacred places.

Those, at least, were my first sensations as I stepped into

the nave. There, I halted in simple admiration of its unexpected magnificence. Atherton had in some measure prepared me, of course, but I was nonetheless taken aback by the beauty of the place. On either side stretched rows of slender piers, alternately circular and octagonal, lifting pointed arches. As I raised my eyes, the whole effect was repeated in the tall arched windows of the clerestory.

I took my time, examining everything I could before moving on, not knowing quite what I was looking for, yet dimly expecting at every moment to sense it, to know it as if, all along, I had expected exactly that and nothing else.

Gradually, I could see what had inspired Atherton to embark upon his plan of restoration. Though the fabric of St Stephen's had been largely completed by the end of the Perpendicular period and little altered since then, and though its interior had been preserved virtually intact through the vandalism of the Commonwealth, it was nonetheless evident that time and fashion had done much to alter its original aspect and make drab or incongruous what had once been so harmonious.

The chancel screen, though still in place, was topped, not by its original rood cross, but by the coat of arms of Queen Elizabeth. In three or four places, painted commandment boards done in the same reign, and other boards with various specimens of holy writ, obscured earlier and finer embellishments. Higher up, coated with dust and shabby among scraps of regimental colours, diamond-shaped hatchments hung as stark reminders of dead nobility.

Beyond these accretions, most of them easily enough got rid of, there were less welcome signs of decay. Stonework had crumbled in places, plaster had fallen, gilt had been eroded, woodwork had succumbed to damp and worms. There lay over St Stephen's church an air of benign neglect, as though all down the years its congregations had entered it in a state of trance, not quite seeing, not quite hearing, while all around them the fabric of the place dwindled and grew ragged at the edges,

Near the chancel, where the altar stood, someone had long ago hung a plain board, on which words from Scripture had been painted in black edged with gold, the latter now much tarnished: 'If they hear not Moſes and the prophets, neither will they be perſwaded, though one roſe from the dead.' I stood a long time in contemplation of this curious object, whose text every eye must have traced Sunday after Sunday, through the long hours of the weekly sermon, and I wondered why it had been hung in such a prominent place.

The chancel stalls were greater in number than might have been expected in a parish church, whose choir can never have been large. I counted ten stalls on the north, another ten on the south, and three each side of the opening at the west end. The stalls were fitted with misericords carved in the form of grotesque faces, some amusing, others faintly disturbing. One I particularly noticed was situated towards the east end of the choir, a monk's head, cowled, with a low forehead and deep-set eyes.

It was there, in the chancel, that I set eyes at last on William de Lindesey's tomb, as though, all along, it had been waiting for me in that waxy silence. I could not have mistaken it, of course, among the eight or nine tombs that jostled for their share of sanctity within the chancel walls. It stood close by the altar rail, a wretched thing draped in a stained tarpaulin.

There was no sign of the wooden winch or the trestles that had been brought in on Atherton's instructions to raise and carry the lid. No doubt Cowper the stonemason had reckoned it unlikely he would need them again, and even more unlikely he would find men willing to operate it within a mile of St Stephen's Church after the accident that had taken Ezekiel Finch's life. For my part, I regretted the winch's absence, since I was sure it would be essential to restore the lid to its original position.

I glanced nervously about me. Atherton and Lethaby were, I knew, somewhere in the vicinity, but I could neither see nor hear them, and I felt very much as though I stood alone in that sequestered place. A dim morning light came sullenly through the tall east window, casting half lights and impressions that were not quite shadows. I coughed once, and the sound echoed a moment or two among the naked stones, then vanished into the vast space beneath the roof. Looking up, I followed the tracery of the ceiling, the play of light and shadow across the stone, and for a fleeting instant I had a feeling that I was being watched.

My hand shook as I took the edge of the tarpaulin and pulled it gingerly from the tomb. It was not that I expected any sudden manifestation, any physical expression of last night's evil; I merely knew that I had come upon a work of immense despair, something I did not, as yet, understand, but which I feared as though I had understood it perfectly.

The lid had been left where it had been dropped when the accident happened. Thankfully, it had not been moved far, and was in no danger of toppling. I glanced uneasily at the gap between it and the wall of the tomb-chest, then turned my attention to the lid itself.

Where one might have expected to find the effigy of a knight in armour or his wife in her best robes, here instead was the cowled figure of a monk, elevated only partly above the flat surface of the tomb, and set inside thin shafts beneath a trefoiled canopy.* Such a tomb is, of course, extremely unusual and much against monastic principles, but I think I understand it now. Why it was designed in that fashion, why it was there at all.

Around the trefoiled canopy the sculptor had carved de Lindesey's name in full, with the date of his death, 8 November 1359. On each of the four sides of the tomb, Latin inscriptions had been incised in elegant Gothic letters, each one a biblical verse (in whole or in part), but curiously chosen, and with a logic (if logic it may be called) that quite defeated me.

On the west and east sides were the following, whose meaning was reasonably clear (or so I then thought): *In tenebris stravi lectulum meum:* 'I have made my bed in the darkness' and *Conlocavit me in obscuris*: 'He hath made me to dwell in darkness'. Beneath the first of these was a verse that occurs twice in the Book of Ruth: 'To raise up the name of the dead upon his inheritance', and beneath the second 'it watcheth for thee; behold, it is come'. Of these two latter inscriptions, I could make no sense.

Beneath these, but set in a quite separate panel that ran all the way along the bottom of the tomb-chest, was what seemed at first to be a lengthy inscription. I bent down to read it, only

---

* It was only a year or so afterwards that I remarked the resemblance between this figure and that of Bishop Kilkenny on the latter's tomb in the north chancel aisle of Ely cathedral. This correspondence, I subsequently learned, had already been noted by Canon Wilfred Thomas in his *Monuments of the Fen Churches* (p. 275): 'The conceit of angels hovering in the spandrels on either side of the canopy recurs as a motif in the altar-tomb of Abbot William de Lindesey in the parish church of Thornham St Stephen, and we may conclude on the basis of both dating and style the work of a single hand.'

to find myself unable to make any sense of it at all. My first thought was that it had been written in a language unknown to me, but it rapidly became clear that what I was reading was, in fact, some sort of code in which the letters had been jumbled up and set down wholly out of order. I tried the most obvious permutations – every other letter, every other letter backwards, substituting for each letter the one before or after it in the alphabet, but all without success.

In the end, I simply wrote the whole thing down, starting at the western end of the south side and working my way round to the beginning – though I had, in truth, as little idea of where the inscription began and ended than I had of what it meant. Strung together, the letters – or, rather, clusters of letters – appeared like this:

BCLDE*LALANIH*OHLELD*OELALDH*
OHDMH*QHALHB*IILCD*MHLGC*BMIOBLD
*LIMFEI*HBLBLI*OGGDLLA

I had scarcely finished this tedious task when I heard a sound behind me. Turning, I saw Atherton and Lethaby approaching from the choir. Atherton seemed grave, but there lay perched on Lethaby's face the most sanctimonious of smiles.

"I see you have found the wicked abbot's tomb," he said, smirking all the while like some species of monkey newly arrived from Madagascar.

"Why do you call him that?" I asked.

He shrugged and smirked again, a monkey still, but very tame and well-mannered, bred not for a circus but a gentleman's shoulder.

"I've heard the locals call him that," he said. "The tomb has an evil reputation hereabouts. The Reverend Atherton had no end of trouble finding men willing to work on it. And now, of course . . . Well, it's too bad. I don't imagine we'll ever finish the repair now. I shall have to bring men in from outside to close it up again."

"You imply the abbot himself has something of a reputation."

He nodded.

"So I understand. It's not a matter I've ever enquired into. No doubt there are local historians who could further enlighten you. Jowett in March, for example – I'm told he has made a study of ecclesiastical institutions in that period. All I know for certain is that the abbey would not have William's body for burial, hence his rather unusual interment here. There are some who say he had dealings with the devil, though I think that somewhat far-fetched."

"Indeed," I said. Atherton caught my eye. 'Far-fetched' was a word he himself might have used the morning before; but not now.

Lethaby took a half-hunter from his pocket and glanced at it.

"It's almost time for our service to start," he said. "If you gentlemen will excuse me, there are one or two preparations I need to make."

He vanished in the direction of the vestry, leaving us together in the abominable silence of the chancel.

"Come," I said. "This is no place to stay."

We turned and headed back towards the choir. As we did so, I heard a sound behind me, repeated two or three times: the sound of scratching against stone. I looked round, but there was nothing there that I could see.

Ten

I was at that time still engaged in writing my study of the Albigensians of Ariège and Languedoc, a work with which I had been occupied for several years, and which was now nearing completion.* My accident and the various incidents of the Christmas vacation had been severe distractions from my work, and I was growing uneasy by the speed with which the deadline for the book was approaching. The start of Lent term and the resumption of my tutorial and professional responsibilities ate yet more deeply into my free time, and for the next few months I kept pretty much to my rooms.

I did not seek out Atherton, nor he me. We met once or twice at university functions, but neither spoke of the events that had brought us so close in the vacation; I sensed that he wished to regard the entire episode as a closed book. He had not been back to Thornham St Stephen, nor did he appear to have kept in touch with Lethaby.

For my own part, I had no wish to return to the village. I did,

---

* Subsequently published as *The Cathar Heresy and the Albigensian Crusades*, London, The Canterbury Press, 1894. Among reviews, see Hippolyte du Puigandeau, *Revue des Études Historiques*, LXI, pp. 347–52; A. De Groot, *Mededeelingen der koninklijke akademie van wetenschappen*, afd. Letterkunde, 26, serie A, no. 2, pp. 74–77.

however, have misgivings about leaving matters as they stood, and in late January I wrote to a churchman of my acquaintance – his name and place of residence need not be recorded in these pages – and asked him to take what steps he reasonably could to settle what had been disturbed. He replied some months later, saying he had spoken with friends at Ely cathedral, and that certain prayers had been said at Thornham St Stephen before William de Lindesey's tomb had been resealed. I wrote him a letter of thanks, made a contribution to a charitable fund over which he has charge, and fervently hoped the matter was closed.

I spent that summer in the south of France, mainly in the *département* of Ariège, the medieval Comté de Foix, roughly corresponding to the diocese of Pamiers. I had been visiting the region for several years, investigating the Cathar villages of the northern Pyrenées between Toulouse and the Spanish border, in order to gather materials for my book, and I wanted to make some final researches in local archives before sending the completed manuscript to press. My leg had healed tolerably well by then, and I was able to get about with only a little difficulty, aided by a stout stick I bought from a local shepherd. The work went well, and, for reasons that I shall explain, I did not return to Cambridge until late September.

Among the letters waiting for me at the porter's lodge was one from Atherton. He apologised for having been so little in touch since our return from Thornham St Stephen, and reiterated his gratitude for my intervention.

"I regret, however," he went on, "that matters have not rested as we left them. I do not speak of Thornham St Stephen, but of my brother. He was, as you know, buried in the cathedral churchyard at my mother's insistence, though near my father, not in the same grave. We had a headstone erected as soon as the grave settled, a fine slab of Purbeck marble. And we thought my brother was at rest.

"It seems now that he was not. My mother has seen him night after night in her dreams, and twice now waking. My dear Asquith, you must understand that my mother is a woman of not inconsiderable sense, not readily given to fanciful thoughts. I have never known her to speak of ghosts or spirits, she quite ridicules the Spiritualists, she has no time for table-rapping. But she has seen my brother.

"I have seen him too, of that I am certain. It was some weeks after his burial, and I was in my college rooms, washing before dinner. I looked up at the mirror to comb my whiskers, and as I did so I saw my brother's figure reflected, as though he was standing at the back of the room by the bookcase, watching me silently. When I turned, he was not there, but I know I saw him. He looked pale and tired, as though hounded by something.

"My mother knows nothing of the events at the rectory. I have said not a word to her, nor do I intend to. It would be needlessly cruel. Nevertheless, she says my brother is not at peace and asks me to do whatever I think needful to restore him to sleep.

"You know more of these matters than I can ever hope to learn, and you have a degree of experience I cannot possibly rival. Will you at least meet my mother and determine for yourself what measure of truth there may be in all this? And will you, for my brother's sake, come with me to the cathedral church-yard at Ely? There is something there that I think you should see."

I did not reply to Atherton at once. This was not a matter I could afford to be further involved in. My deadline was pressing hard, my name had been proposed and accepted for membership on one or two important academic committees, and the sudden illness of one of my colleagues meant that my teaching duties for Michaelmas term would be more onerous than usual.

I had, above all, a single, overriding reason for not wishing to be drawn more deeply into so perilous a business. While in France, I had stayed at the home of René Seillière, a local historian of some eminence, with whom I had corresponded regularly for several years. René and I had developed a close friendship, in part through our correspondence, and more recently when I had stayed with him and his wife during my visits to the Pyrenées.

The Seillières lived sixty miles south of Toulouse, in the small village of St Barthélemy, where René combined the job of schoolmaster with that of *receveur des postes*. I had always found his company congenial and his erudition beyond reproach, and I looked forward to my visit with very real enthusiasm, touched with some sadness, for I knew that my future researches were likely to keep me within the confines of England.

On my arrival, I found René in lower spirits than was customary, and his wife similarly afflicted. On enquiring after the cause of their distress, I was told that their only daughter, Simone, had been suddenly widowed several months earlier and left to fend for herself with a young child, a boy of seven named Bertrand. Mother and child had been living with the Seillières since shortly after her husband's death, and, while the old couple rejoiced in their daughter's company and the bright spirits of their grandson, they were dismayed to find Simone still disconsolate and, it seemed, unable to come to terms with her new situation. She had been married only eight years, and was herself now only twenty-six years of age. Since her marriage eight years earlier, she had been living in the hilltop town of St Bertrand-de-Comminges, where her husband, Marcellin, had worked as a veterinary surgeon.

A Shadow on the Wall

The first evening, at dinner, I met Simone for the first time. I had not really been prepared for what I saw. Perhaps I had imagined a widow in black weeds, older than her years, a little bent and gaunt with grief. Or a younger version of her mother, rather plump and inoffensive, a motherly woman disinclined to speech. But Simone was none of those, that I could see at once. She was pale, certainly – almost extravagantly so, and thin too; but it seemed to me that she must always have been pale and always thin, that these were not the products of grief so much as nature. And her face was quite beyond belief, with dark, moist eyes that absorbed me all night in admiration.

True, she spoke very little, but not, I sensed, because she had nothing to say or thought her opinions not worth airing, but because something had died a little in her and would not easily be reborn.

It was proposed that Simone should accompany me on my peregrinations about the countryside, partly because she would be an excellent guide, and partly – so my good friend René confided to me – because it was felt the occupation might help take her a little out of herself. And so it was that we spent most days in one another's company, when work at home was not too pressing, or Bertrand too demanding.

I did not think, when first we set out together, that I would fall in love with her, but I did. And for over a month I concealed my feelings, for I could not imagine she would ever reciprocate the passion of a dry stick of a man like me, nearly twice her age, a man who had spent all his life among books and manuscripts. It was enough for me that we got on so well, that we were so entirely satisfied in one another's company. We would talk as we wandered down the goat tracks and faint paths that connected one village to the next, or share our thoughts over a glass of wine as we prepared to set off home at the end of the day. So great, indeed, was my pleasure in her being there, and my dejection whenever she was not, that I failed to see that she was slowly changing in her manner towards me, as much as I towards her.

There was perhaps a week remaining to the date of my proposed departure, for I planned to return to Paris at the end of August in order to prosecute certain vital enquiries in the Bibliothèque Nationale. Simone and I had gone together to Montaillou, a small place whose entire population had been arrested and charged with heresy in 1308 by Geoffroy d'Ablis, the Inquisitor of Carcassonne, and again ten years and more later under the Inquisition of Jacques Fournier, then Bishop of Pamiers.* Something of the mood of the old heresy hunts still lingers in the place, for it is sombre and on guard against the outside world, and I did not feel myself altogether welcome there.

Simone was quiet all that day, and as we made our way back she would not reply to my remarks and questions with more than a 'yes' or 'no'. I asked her in the end what was the matter. She merely stopped and shook her head at first, then looked at me and said she was oppressed by the thought of my leaving. A younger man, or one more experienced in dealing with women, might have sensed at once what was wrong, or guessed it long before that. I simply told her I too was sad to be going, and we started on our way again. But she was still taciturn, and at last I stopped again and asked her why it should trouble her so much, for I had surely become an intolerable burden to her family, and a great nuisance to her, with my incessant excursions into the most remote parts of the mountains.

---

* This is the same Fournier who was made a cardinal in 1327 and elected Pope of Avignon in 1334 under the name Benedict XII. He was a lifelong opponent of heresy, counting among his opponents such illustrious names as Giacomo dei Fiori, Meister Eckhart and Occam.

I had meant all this in jest, but Simone took it to heart and shook her head and protested. Moments later, she was in my arms, blurting out her secret to me, red-faced and trembling. I was stunned and unable to move or speak for fear I might shatter the beauty of that moment. But I held her tightly, as if she were a puff of smoke that might drift away, and when I looked down at her, I told her what was in my own heart, holding back nothing.

Well, I shall not draw this out. We were engaged that same evening, and no one less surprised than her father and mother, who said they had suspected something of the sort long before Simone or I had grown aware of how things stood. As a result, I stayed a fortnight longer in St Barthélemy than I had planned, though now it was to spend time with Simone in the house, to talk with her and get to know her and little Bertrand.

Her parents thought that, anxious though we were to be married, the wedding should not take place until a full twelvemonth had elapsed from the date of Simone's husband's death, and to this plan we reluctantly gave our consent. I could not much longer put off my journey to Paris, for my work there was pressing and my time severely limited. We therefore concluded that I should leave alone and, my labours once completed, make my way back to Cambridge, there to await Simone's arrival, accompanied by her mother, Albertine, and Bertrand.

So it was that Atherton's letter reached me at a far from suitable time. I expected my fiancée any day, and the thought of being occupied in such a dark business at the time of her arrival filled me with the greatest distaste.

Before I had time to reply to him, however, a letter reached me from René, saying that Bertrand had been taken ill with a slight fever, and that Simone's departure must be postponed until he was fully recovered and fit to travel. That letter was followed in the very next post by another from Simone herself, in which she poured out such loving sentiments that I almost blessed the delay that had been the occasion of her writing them.

At all events, I was much cast down by this news, though not as yet disposed to return anything but an unfavourable response to Atherton's appeal. The next day, however, brought a second letter in his hand, in which his urgings were not merely renewed, but given added force by the news that his mother had fallen seriously ill and was not expected to survive above three or four days.

"Please hurry," he wrote, "for she begs you to come. Her condition is perilous, but her mind lucid and her wishes perfectly clear, namely that she must at all costs consult you in this matter before she dies. Indeed, I think her fear of death has become very great, and she will not be easy in her mind until she has spoken with you and received certain assurances. I must remain with her, but I urge you to make all possible haste." I confess I still hesitated for a couple of hours, torn between my reluctance to have any more to do with Atherton's fiend and my sense of duty to a man who had never harmed me in any way. In the end, my conscience goaded me so severely that I went to the post office and sent a telegram to Atherton, asking him to meet me off the next train. I remembered how I had set aside Atherton's last appeal, and with what consequences. This time I should at least be on hand to offer his dying mother whatever solace I had to give.

Mrs Atherton lived at Abbeystead, the house to which she had retired on her husband's death some eight years earlier. It was situated at some distance from Wilburton, a village a few miles south of Ely. The house itself is on Wilburton Fen, between the Catch-Water Drain and the Old West River. There is a branch line of the Norfolk Railway running there from Ely once or twice a day. I informed Atherton that I would take the 3.10 train to Ely and make my way to Wilburton on a train that left shortly after four.

To my surprise, he was waiting for me at Ely with a dogcart. "I'm very glad to see you," he said.

"I didn't expect to see you here," I replied. I smiled and shook his hand as I jumped up, though I could not wholly echo his sentiments. I liked the man well enough, but he awakened in me such unwelcome associations that, in all honesty, I should have preferred to see as little of him as possible.

"Mother knows you're coming," he said. "But her strength has been somewhat low all day. Dr Hastings says she must rest a little. She may receive you this evening if her sleep restores her sufficiently."

"I'm content to wait."

"Well," he said, flicking the whip lightly as we moved away, "it is perhaps fortunate. We can make excellent use of the time. I told you there was something I wished to show you here at Ely. That's why I decided to meet you here instead of Wilburton. With your permission, I'd like to take you there now. It will be better if you have seen it for yourself before you meet my mother."

"Won't you tell me what it is?"

He shook his head and clucked gently to the horse.

"I'd rather you reached your own conclusions," he said. "We don't have far to go."

In a couple of minutes we had reached the cathedral, its vast bulk unmissable above every rooftop. A shaft of light from the setting sun caught the octagon as we approached, then as quickly shuffled back behind a cloud. Autumn was thick in the air, a cool breeze had come in uninterrupted from the sea, and the first leaves had started to fall. Somewhere, a bonfire was burning, imprinting the evening air with woodsmoke.

Atherton tied up the dogcart and led me to the churchyard. It was growing dark, but he had come prepared with a lantern. In the fading light, we made our way between the graves until we came at last to his brother's tombstone, a low marble stone set at the foot of a yew tree, and not far from the wall of the cathedral. I bent down and read the inscription.

Rev. Edward Atherton M.A., D.D.
10 March 1832 – 3 January 1883
Sometime Rector of the Parish of Thornham St Stephen
'Therefore we are buried with him
by baptism into death:
that like as Christ was raised up from the dead
by the glory of the Father
even so we also should walk in newness of life.'
Rom. VI:4
R.I.P.

"My mother chose the verse," said Atherton. He stood beside me, shivering slightly in the chill wind.

The words were finely cut, sharp and deep in the face of the new stone. But a delicate film of moss had already blurred the bottom half of the inscription, and the grave itself was looking bedraggled and ill-tended.

"Does no one come here often?" I asked.

Atherton shook his head.

"My mother did in the beginning. But she stopped some months ago, when . . ."

"What is it? What did you want to show me?"

In answer, he pointed to the stone.

"Take a closer look," he said.

I bent down, bringing my face close to the headstone. As I did so, I noticed, faint beneath the layer of moss, what seemed to be a tracing of another inscription. With my bare hand I wiped some of the moss clear, then peered closely at the stone. There were indeed letters, not cut by any chisel, but somehow apparent in the marble as though by the action of some intense stain, or a discoloration rising out of the stone itself.

EVIGILAVIT ADVERSUM TE ECCE VENIT

"It's from the Book of Ezekiel," prompted Atherton. "'It watcheth for thee; behold, it is come.'"*

In the west, the sun sank finally, returning the world to darkness. Our lantern seemed a pitiful thing before the force of the coming night. I straightened and looked at Atherton.

"I would like to speak with your mother," I said.

---

* *Euigilabit* in *Amiatinus*, Florence, Bibl. Mediceo-Laurenz; Amiatino, I, s. VIII in. in Northumbria; also in Orléans, Bibl. mun. 17 (14), s. VIII–IX Floriaci.

Eleven

We drove to Wilburton in silence, broken only by the sound of our horse's hooves and the turning of the dogcart's wheels, now on stone, now on grass, now on earth. I had no explanation for the letters that had appeared on Edward Atherton's tombstone, and for the moment I preferred not to let my thoughts dwell on the subject.

Abbeystead is a medium-sized dwelling set in an isolated part of the fens. The Hoghill Drove lies to its west, and the Twenty-pence to the east, and all in between is open and bleak and swept by cold winds all winter long. The house itself seems eminently suited to a bishop's widow, being neither too luxurious nor unduly spartan. A fine red-brick house with five straight gables, it dates back to the seventeenth century, and has, I understand, been in Mrs Atherton's family since the eighteenth.

The doctor was there when we arrived, this being his second visit of the day. He took Atherton aside into the little library, and talked earnestly with him before taking his leave.

"Hastings says Mother has recovered somewhat, but that we must not tire her. No doubt the nurse will pitch us out if we go on too long. Would you like to eat before we go up?"

I shook my head. Mrs Atherton might well relapse if we left it too long.

We went directly to her bedroom, our feet unconsciously soft on the stairs, as though fearing to alarm her. The air was pervaded by the scents of candle-wax and lamp oil, for, as in Thornham St Stephen, gas had not yet reached Wilburton, let alone Abbeystead. Flames shivered in a cold draught, and danced in the polished woodwork of the balustrade. Atherton knocked on his mother's door, and moments later the nurse let us in. She was young and pleasant-faced, with the efficient manner of someone trained in one of the new teaching hospitals.

The room was in darkness, save for a lamp on the table to the left of the bed, where the nurse had been sitting. A smell of carbolic soap and strong medicine filled the air, mixing with the odours of lamp oil and burning logs to create the unmistakable, dreary scent of a sick-room.

"She's more herself, sir," whispered the nurse, "but still sinking."

"This is the gentleman she expressed a desire to see. Is it all right if he speaks with her now?"

"That's all right, sir, but Dr Hastings says she mustn't be kept talking long, and you'll excuse me if I see she's not distressed."

Atherton ushered me forward. The old lady was propped up against a sea of pillows, all encased in voluminous white lace. A lace cap was tied round her head, and from it long strands of white hair spilled out across the pillows like foam. All this whiteness served as a sort of frame to hold a face almost as white, and the face in turn framed a pair of eyes like faded coral.

"Mother, this is Professor Asquith. He has come from Cambridge specially to see you."

The trace of a smile crossed the half-dead lips, and the

old woman motioned faintly with her right hand. I crossed to the nurse's chair and sat down. Asquith stood alongside me, gazing down at his mother with an anxious expression, as though expecting her to depart this life at any moment.

"I'm sorry to have . . . brought you all this way . . . for so little, Professor," the old lady began. Her voice, though weak, was clear enough, and I sensed behind it a strength of will that had not altogether deserted her.

"The sick are not to be denied," I said. "I am pleased to be here."

"I fear you do not find me . . . sick . . . but dying."

I began to perceive how with each word she struggled to speak something imperceptible went out of her. I waited, saying nothing. Her eyes held me steady. I knew she could see me clearly, and I knew I was not all she saw.

"I was never . . . afraid of death before," she continued. "I have . . . lived a long life . . . and I have always . . . known the comfort of the Church . . . But since my son Edward . . . died, I have known . . . no peace . . . and I have had no comfort.

"Matthew has told me nothing . . . of the circumstances . . . of Edward's death . . . But I . . . guess more than he thinks . . ."

"Mother—" Atherton broke in.

"Keep quiet, Matthew. This is . . . between Professor Asquith . . . and myself." She returned her gaze to me. Every word weakened her, she was determined to make the most of what she said.

"Professor, I am a . . . frightened woman. I have seen my son . . . twice since his death. Each time . . . he has appeared to me . . . terribly changed. He is not . . . in the arms of a . . . loving God. Nor do I think . . . he is in hell. He inhabits a sort of . . . limbo, where he is tormented by something . . . I do not understand. He tells me . . . he said you had freed him . . . but that he was not yet free."

I still said nothing. I knew what she was driving me to.

"He said there is still . . . a great evil . . . at Thornham St Stephen. That it is not at rest . . . He said you must put it to rest . . . that the prayers were not enough . . . I do not understand. Do you?"

I nodded.

"Yes," I whispered. "I understand perfectly."

"And you will do it? You will . . . put this thing to rest."

I hesitated. I thought of Simone, of our coming marriage, of the risks I would be taking. But this was a dying woman, and she was frightened.

"Why did Edward speak to you? Why not to me?"

"He did not know . . . where to find you. I am his mother. He came to me."

"Is he here now?" I asked. "Is he in this room?"

She shifted for the first time, her head uneasy on the sea of pillows, as though suddenly adrift.

"He has been here," she whispered. Her voice was growing faint now, as though receding from us along a thin corridor of death. "But not now . . . not now."

I felt the nurse's hand on my shoulder.

"She needs to rest now," she said. "It's not good to keep her talking."

I took Mrs Atherton's hand in mine and looked into her eyes. They were starting to close, but their gaze still penetrated me.

"Very well," I said, and my heart sank within me. "I shall do what has to be done."

She smiled then, a little girl's smile in an old woman's dying face, and said no more to me, and closed her eyes, which I never saw open again.

*   *   *

Atherton and I dined together alone, for there were no visitors, none being admitted to his mother. He expected relations on the following day, an aunt and some cousins, and friends from the neighbourhood would undoubtedly call, to enquire about his mother's condition, or to bid her a tearful farewell. He himself was prepared for the event; it held few terrors for him.

"I only pray that she will slip away peacefully," he said. "Her life has not been peaceful since my brother died. And she took my father's death very hard before that. I would not see her suffer now."

I said nothing, but thought to myself, if only suffering were all.

"When you saw your brother," I went on, after a brief silence, "was he altered, as your mother found him?"

"He was a little, yes, though not as gravely as she says. But you must remember that I saw him less clearly, and for a shorter time. I am certain he was trying to speak to me, to communicate something: a message, a warning – I'm not sure."

"And did you try to speak to him?"

He hesitated, putting down his knife and fork as though all appetite had suddenly left him.

"No," he said. "I was frightened. There was . . . something in his expression . . ." His voice faltered. "Something hungry . . ."

After dinner, we passed to the library, to drink a little port and talk of books we had recently read. Neither alluded to the true reason for my presence there, whether from politeness or fear I cannot say. In one corner, a clock ticked with flat, precise strokes, and from time to time one or the other of us would look round at it, to see how long had now passed since the last time. Two or three times, Atherton rang for the maid, to ask her to enquire after his mother. Each time, the answer from upstairs was simply, "No change, sir."

At ten o'clock, we retired. I had been given a room near Atherton's, with a wide bed and a pleasant fire. The window overlooked a wide lawn, beyond which lay the fens, bleak and silent under a white moon. I stood by the window for a long time, staring out into the darkness, lost in my own musings. I tried to think of Simone and the life we would begin together, but again and again my thoughts returned to the old woman whose room lay only a few doors from my own, and whose coming death pervaded the house.

The moon slowly changed position, and thin clouds came up from the west, darkening its light. I caught sight of a flickering of dark wings in a clump of trees at the foot of the lawn, then all returned to the stillness in which it had been.

Just then, a deeper shadow caught my eye, something moving slowly a little to my left, just where a dip in the grass led down to a summerhouse. I strained to make out what it was, but though I stood there for some time, I did not see it again. In the end, my eyes grew tired, and I returned to the fireplace.

I undressed, but I found my bed oppressive and sleep impossible. Getting up again, I lit the lamp and sat by the fire, trying to read. The stillness was unbearable. On the mantelpiece, a carriage clock ticked. Outside, an owl screeched twice, then silence fell again. My book lay open on my lap. I had not read a single sentence. Footsteps passed in the hall, a door opened and closed, and the stillness returned. The fire burned down steadily, but I did not add fresh wood. I stared into the embers, thinking of the promise I had made. Somewhere, a clock chimed midnight.

I went to the window and looked out again. A thick mist had drifted in from the fens. I could see nothing clearly. The whole world seemed to be holding its breath. Outside my window, the mist moved dreamily about, now parting, now opening to reveal darkness. I pulled the curtains to and returned to the fire.

It cannot have been more than a minute after I did so when the silence was broken by a loud cry, a long, wrenching cry uttered by someone in mortal terror. I stood at once, my heart thudding unpleasantly, aware that the scream had come from the direction of Mrs Atherton's room.

When I got there, Atherton had just reached the door. I joined him and put my hand on his shoulder.

"Let me go in," I said. No sound came from the room. All I could hear were footsteps downstairs as the house staff came to investigate.

"It's my mother, for God's sake."

"All the more reason. I'll come for you once I've seen everything's all right."

Reluctantly, he stood back and let me go in alone.

The room was almost as I remembered it from my earlier visit. The nurse's lamp still burned on the bedside table. As I stepped through the door, I noticed that a curtain had been pulled back from the window to the right of the bed, and that the window itself had been opened. At the same instant, I became aware that the temperature in the room had dropped, and that a patch of mist lay between the window and the bed. I also observed that the sick-room odour that had been so strong previously had been overlaid by another smell, a most unpleasant stench of decay.

No sooner had I taken notice of these things, than my attention was drawn to the bed. Mrs Atherton lay there as before, but her face no longer had the composed expression of a woman who has made up her mind to die, but rather one of the most agonising terror. Her features had been contorted by fear into a mockery of what I had seen not many hours earlier.

It was immediately obvious to me that she was dead. Nonetheless, I looked round to find the nurse, as though to seek confirmation. At first I could see her nowhere, and thought angrily that she must have deserted her post. And then I looked more closely at the shadows around the foot of her chair, and saw her slumped there, her body limp and twisted.

I rushed across to her and bent down, fearing that she too was dead, and from the same cause. To my relief, I saw she was still breathing, though unconscious. I started to raise her to a sitting position against the bed, and as I did so, I happened to look up directly at the open window on the other side of the room. As long as I live, I shall regret having done so. For I caught a glimpse of something in the mist behind the curtain, a shadowy thing that emerged with a quick motion and made for the opening.

Its image is still vivid on my waking mind, set there like a photograph, though mercifully blurred. In the seconds before it vanished, I saw something tall and stooped and horribly thin, a gangling thing that moved disjointedly, almost like an insect. It wore a tattered habit that barely covered its limbs, and a hood pulled over its head. As it passed through the window, it turned its face to me, and for the briefest of moments I glimpsed its eyes. The next moment, it was gone, and Matthew Atherton was by my side, helping me to my feet.

Twelve

The following week was spent in making arrangements for Atherton's mother's funeral, and settling her affairs. I returned to Cambridge to consider what must next be done, and to devise a strategy for how best to go about it. Atherton stayed at Wilburton all that week, although, at my advice, he stayed with friends in the village, and not at Abbeystead.

Before leaving the house myself, I took care to speak with the nurse, a girl from March called Lily Barnes, and to elicit from her the details of what she had seen and heard the night before. Her story was confused, and her narrative much affected by the very real fear that telling it caused her.

A little before midnight, she had felt inexplicably drowsy. Since falling asleep could lead to her instant dismissal, she took steps to freshen herself, stepping to the window and drawing up the sash, in order to let some cooler air into the room. Having done so, she felt much better, but decided to return to her seat, leaving the curtain drawn and the window a little open.

Not many minutes had passed when she noticed that mist from outside had drifted into the room. At that same moment, she observed that her patient was stirring in her sleep and appeared distressed. Mrs Atherton began to mumble incoherently and showed signs of waking. Lily went to her side, intending to reassure her and to encourage her to return to sleep; as she did so, she happened to glance up at the window, thinking the change in air might have been to blame for the change in the old lady's condition. At the window, she saw a "horrid" figure climbing into the opening. As it straightened and looked at her, she caught sight of its face . . .

"What I mean, sir, is that it didn't exactly have a face. There were eyes, I know that, and something very like a mouth, but it wasn't . . . a face as such . . ."

She remembers nothing after that, poor girl. Her prospects have been much blighted by the experience, for she now refuses to take any night jobs, and is uneasy even to be left alone with a sick patient during daylight hours. I said what I could to encourage her, but it was not much.

In Cambridge, I spent several days in the University Library, sorting through various monastic documents, some printed, some in manuscript, most of them dating from the fourteenth century – cartularies, rolls, chronicles. Though I could not find exactly what I wanted, I was able to form a broader picture than before, and to see more clearly what was missing.

Atherton got back from Wilburton late on the Friday, much worn down by his new-found responsibilities. He had not entered his mother's room until after I closed the window, and I had said nothing to him of what I had seen, and repeated nothing of Lily Barnes's tale. Nonetheless, he was not a man to be easily deceived. I had been unable to prevent him seeing his mother in those terrible moments after her death, and the expression on her face, so similar in all respects to that imprinted on his brother Edward's features, had told him all he needed to know.

He got in touch with me straight away, and we dined that evening at my college before retiring to my rooms to talk. I still thought it prudent to say nothing of the figure the nurse and I had seen, but I told him I believed that William de Lindesey had returned from the grave and that he sought a proper human form in which to resume his existence. Failing that, he would draw strength from others, driving them to their deaths if need be.

"What are we to do?" Atherton asked when I had finished my explanation.

"I must go back to Thornham St Stephen. I'd like you to accompany me. You know Lethaby, and he has, I trust, some respect for you and your family. We shall need his cooperation if we are to do what has to be done. The prayers that were said after your brother's death have not been enough to lay this thing to rest. More than prayers are needed now, but we shall need Lethaby's consent."

"You may find him hard to persuade."

"He has no choice. Not if he wishes to rid his parish of a very great evil."

We set off for Thornham St Stephen the next morning, taking the route we had followed in January. Our journey was without incident, and almost without conversation, for we were both preoccupied. I remember thinking, as we entered the fen country west of March, that the monks had chosen isolated places such as this the better to mortify their carnal selves, and that one of their number had found in solitude a discontent far greater than a city might have bred. The fields were sere and turning barren. Above them, the grey sky was empty of birds. We were like scarecrows, passing through that emptiness alone.

Lethaby had been alerted to our arrival by a telegram sent ahead early that morning. He was waiting for us at the rectory, and, from the look of him when we were shown into his study, none too pleased to set eyes on us.

"You'll forgive me," he said, "if I don't stand. I have a touch of gout, extremely painful. My father had it before me, he was most unwell of it."

Atherton bent, stretching out his hand.

"Sorry to hear of your affliction. I would have thought you young for such a complaint." He straightened. "You remember Professor Asquith, of course."

Lethaby shook my hand, then motioned us to sit down. His manner was all politeness, his demeanour betrayed something less than cordiality. I had seen the church from the dogcart as we approached the village, I was feeling ill at ease. To be here again. To be so close. In my imagination, I could feel his breath on me, wet and ill-smelling.

I explained in as short a fashion as possible why we had come. Lethaby listened, his expression unchanging. I could sense the incredulity, but, more than that, the smooth working of an instinct for self-preservation. When I came to a close, he sat for some time in silence, watching me.

"Professor," he said finally, "I cannot say how disappointed I am in you. When we first met, I already knew your reputation as a man of science. I hardly thought you a table-rapper."

"Mr Lethaby, this is a serious matter. I would not come to you if it were not."

"Serious? It is the most laughable thing I have heard in a long time. Besides, even were I to humour you and Mr Atherton here, I should have to seek the dean's permission, and he, very likely, the bishop's. I will tell you now that under no circumstances am I willing to jeopardise my standing in their eyes for the sake of something so trivial."

Atherton made to rise, and I thought he would strike Lethaby. I held his arm and whispered to him to be still.

"I'm sorry you regard this matter in so poor a light," I said to Lethaby. "I assure you I do not." I paused. "Tell me, how have things gone in Thornham St Stephen since I was here last? Have there been many deaths? Many sicknesses? Disturbances?"

For a moment, Lethaby's face seemed to turn pale. He did not answer right away. When he did, his words were carefully chosen.

"Some deaths, yes, of course. Winter always takes away a few of our oldest. And some not so old."

"Children?"

He nodded.

"Yes, that was most unexpected. And others ill. It has been a worrying year."

"And you still refuse to listen to what I am telling you?"

He struggled for some moments, for I fancy the better part of him knew I was telling the truth, then regained control.

"There can be no connection between our tragedies and what you have told me. This is not the Middle Ages, Professor. Perhaps you have spent too much time studying the period, perhaps you have started to think like a medieval priest. For my part, I consider myself a modern churchman, and I regard it my duty to combat superstition in any form. You will excuse me, but I have a parish to attend to."

I did not try to argue. He was beyond my reach. The way back to Cambridge was drab, and we did not speak for most of it.

On my return, I found a telegram waiting for me at the porters' lodge. It was from Simone, saying that Bertrand had made an excellent recovery, and that they would all arrive on the Tuesday of the following week, if that was acceptable.

The following day, I had a letter from her, in which she explained that her father had received several new pupils to board with him, and that her mother could not be spared after all to remain in Cambridge until it was time for the wedding. My heart sank as I read these words, only to soar again as I came to what followed. Rather than endure too long an interval before we could be married, she had persuaded her father to agree to hire a deputy for a few weeks, so the family could travel to Cambridge. We could be married as soon as the wedding could be arranged, for we had never meant it to be anything more than a small affair.

My happiness at this news can scarcely be imagined. I at once set about making arrangements: accommodation had to be found for the Seillières, I had to apply for a marriage licence and fix a date for us to be married by a Catholic priest, and, above all, I had to find a house for us to rent, into which we could move after the wedding. The wedding was to be a quiet affair, with the Seillières and some of my family and friends. Of a reception and honeymoon I had not thought: all that mattered to me then was to be with Simone again.

Thirteen

Thornham St Stephen was not forgotten. I had made my promise to Mrs Atherton, and I considered myself held by it. Before Simone's arrival, I did two things. I wrote again to my friend the churchman, and I spent several days in the cathedral library at Ely, reading the records that had been stored there since the dissolution of Thornham Abbey.

William de Lindesey became abbot there in the year 1345, at the age of fifty, having been at various times precentor, claustral prior, and sub-prior in the main monastery, and abbot's provost at the daughter establishment at Thornham St Stephen, from which he was recalled to take up his abbacy.*

According to the fifteenth-century Latin chronicle from which this information is taken, the *Historia de rebus gestis Tornhamiensibus*, William was a tall man, forbidding of appearance, and reputed for his sternness,† yet zealous in his devotions and renowned for his intelligence and learning.

---

* *Revocatus et pro summe religionis industria Tornhame abbas effectus est.*

†*Inobedientibus et indisciplinatis rigidum se et severum exhiberet.*

He came of a noble family long resident near Cambridge, and it seems that he spent some years at the not long-established university there, from which, it is rumoured, he was expelled in some disgrace. The details are not known.

After Cambridge, he spent some time in France, where he entered a convent of black monks at Fleury in the Loire valley. It was there that he completed his noviciate, and from there that he was sent back to England, first to Abingdon in Berkshire, and finally to Thornham.

A cellarer's roll from the abbey itself and a record of an episcopal visitation in 1352 told me that William's abbacy coincided with the virtual elimination of his monastic community by disease.

The Black Death reached East Anglia in March 1349, and continued there until the autumn. In those few months, it wrought extensive havoc throughout the region, with greater numbers succumbing there than in most other parts of the kingdom. No town, village, bailiwick, or abbey was spared. Thornham Abbey was almost wiped out. Of the fifty-four monks living there before the plague, a mere dozen or so remained when it had passed. Its sixty-two lay brethren were reduced in a matter of months to fewer than twenty.

The Bishop of Ely had been at Avignon in France when the plague struck at home. He did not return until the scourge had passed. In his absence, the affairs of the diocese were managed by first five, then eight Vicars-General, but they could barely hold together a system everywhere shaken by sudden death and an all-pervading loss of faith.

At Thornham, Abbot William struggled to do all in his power to hold out against the forces of disintegration. Eight times a day, at the appointed hours, he summoned his dwindling community to the divine office. Each day another one or two or three well-loved faces would be missing from the choir. Nonetheless, William refused to let his monks give in to despair. The offering up of prayers continued, in spite of every indication that God had abandoned His children, or, worse still, that it was His hand that laid waste the countryside.

So long as prayer continued, so did the provision of hospitality to any who sought shelter within the monastery walls. William issued firm instructions that none were to be turned away, though it was thought by some that travellers brought the pestilence with them. He ordered an inscription erected above the abbey gate: *Porta patens esto, nulli claudaris honesto* – 'Gate be open, shut to no honest person.' And, indeed, there was no shortage of honest men, women, and children who, abandoning their homes and their allegiances, sought safety from God's vengeance behind the abbey walls.

Reading thus far, I could not but be impressed by William and the fortitude with which he led his people through their darkest hour. As far as I could see, the Abbot of Thornham had been near enough a saint, maintaining faith in his God in the midst of universal despair, and extending charity to others regardless of the cost. I almost admired him. But I knew that something had come between the good abbot and his soul, that some darkness greater even than the plague had descended on him. So I read further, and at last I came across a hint of what that darkness might have been.

At the height of the pestilence, when it seemed the dying and burying would have no end, there arrived at Thornham Abbey a knight from Norfolk, Sir Hugh de Warenne, accompanied by his wife Margaret and some others of his household, ten in all. Sir Hugh and his wife, who appears to have been related to William, sought and were granted lodging in the abbot's house.

The Latin chronicler records this event in a mere three lines, ending with the melancholy notice that all save one of Sir Hugh's party perished within a month and were buried together in the plague pit dug outside the abbey walls. Sir Hugh and his wife, however, survived the plague and left Thornham late that autumn, but it is not clear where they went from there, for other records show that they did not return to Norfolk.

There is, however, an earlier document, an anonymous daily record of the plague kept by a monk who lived through those dreadful times. This narrative has no title, for it lacks several folios from both front and rear. A note attached to it says it was discovered by a party of suppression commissioners searching for treasure at the time of the abbey's dissolution, having been hidden behind a loose brick in the monks' dorter. I came across it only by accident, in the last hours I spent at Ely.

The chronicle seems to be part of a longer record, for it begins with events in the year before the plague, 1348, while a few pages at the end are taken up with the first months of 1350.

In thys yeare, begins the account for 1349, *cam ther to Thornam pestilence, also al maner of folk for to scapen therfro.*

For the most part, it is a bald enough chronicle, but the section dealing with the plague makes harrowing reading, for tiny details serve to make individual and poignant what might otherwise have been merely routine. "There died today Brother John, the cellarer, he that was so witty and told such tales at Christmastide", "there followed him Brother Thomas, whose complexion was like a girl's, and whose manner was as soft", "Brother Edmund, who ate three men's fill when he was able", "a girl-child of five who had that very morning been playing with her doll".

When he comes to the arrival of Sir Hugh de Warenne, he breaks from his narrative to enter into greater detail. It is perfectly obvious that our author must have occupied a position which gave him access to the abbot's lodging throughout the month or so that Hugh and his wife were resident there, for he writes as one who has seen much with his own eyes. He was very likely William's chaplain or seneschal, and, as such, a reliable source.

This Hugh of Warenne possesses lands in fief from the Duke of Norfolk, chiefly a great estate by Wymondham. He is a proud man, exceeding haughty of demeanour, and much given to comment on his station and his name, which he holds in the highest esteem. His wife, Dame Margaret, that keeps close to him at all times, and will not be parted from him, is in no way inferior to her husband in disdaining all that are not high born. The lord abbot alone will she speak with, for he is a kinsman of hers, and of noble birth.

They arrived yesterday between Sext and None, it being the sixteenth day of July. I saw them as they entered the abbot's lodging. Both Sir Hugh and his wife showed signs of great fear and perturbation. The plague rages at Norwich and in the countryside all about, and they have left their estate in order to find a refuge here among men of God. Safety they are not likely to find, but, God willing, they will die with the rest of us absolved of their sins.

They spent above an hour cloistered with my lord abbot, and I observed on their leaving that all traces of fear had left their faces. Others who saw them at this time deemed it the work of divine grace through the person of Abbot William. I pray that it is so, but fear some other explanation. The abbot was preoccupied all that night and would not speak to me more than six words. He does not seem at peace.

Three men of Sir Hugh's entourage arrived with the first

signs of the illness already on them. They spent the first night in the lay brothers' dorter, but yesterday were transferred to the lay infirmary. One has large buboes in his groin, and is in much discomfort, groaning constantly. Neither lord nor lady has visited any of them.

This evening when we dined, I overheard Sir Hugh ask my lord abbot if 'that which he had brought' was safe. Abbot William coloured and nodded quickly, like one who will not speak of a matter openly. I was reminded of occasions in the past when he had shown himself likewise secretive. There are, I have long suspected, matters in his life that he would not wish to have disclosed. Of his time in France particularly, he has never spoken to me, and my questions regarding the abbey there have gone unanswered . . .

The sickest of the three men died this morning after Prime. His name was Wilfrid, and he had been Sir Hughe's reeve at Wymondham. We prayed for his soul during the sung mass at Terce, and those of his companions who were still in health attended in the nave, but neither his liege lord nor his lady was to be seen . . .

Two more of Sir Hugh's men have fallen ill, and another died today. I discovered that one of the sick men, Thomas of Worstead, had served as his master's secretary, and I therefore paid him a visit in the infirmary, with the consent of the lay infirmarer. We had long converse, and Thomas held nothing back, for he knows he is to die. Nothing befits the dying more than honesty, and what was said to me was in part a confession, for which I gave him absolution.

Sir Hugh has a bad reputation in his own region, and

his lady as bad or worse. There are those who say he has had converse with the devil, and entertained sorcerers and Mahometans in his house.

His grandfather, Sir Godfrey de Warenne, accompanied Prince Edward on his crusade against the Saracen, and it is said he remained in the land of Outremer long after Edward's return, until the fall of Acre.

This Sir Godfrey travelled back to England by way of Italy and France, and brought with him books and treasure that he had taken from the infidel, and a Saracen servant, whose name men say was Mahound, like the false prophet. All this passed in time to Sir Godfrey's son, Edmund, and from him to Hugh, the same that is even now with us.

Now, when the pestilence came to Norwich, some said the Jews had brought it, and some the lepers. But others, among them canons of the cathedral, were of the opinion that the cause of this disease was none but Sir Hugh de Warenne and his ungodliness. As the dead grew daily in number and the sick multiplied, so the voices calling for Sir Hugh's arrest waxed ever louder, until they would not be stifled.

But word of this had by then reached to Wymondham, and Sir Hugh decided to flee the mob's fury and seek refuge here at Thornham. He brought with him his wife and his closest retainers, also a chest containing, Thomas believed, a relic from Jerusalem – though whether it is a saint's bones or the head of a martyr or a virgin's shift, he knows not . . .

Thomas of Worstead died today in great pain, and in terror that he be judged for having served so evil a master. I was with him when he died, but all he said was raving, save one thing: that he had seen a shadow on the wall where no shadow should have been, and that he was afraid. I signed him with the cross then, and myself likewise. But he did not die at peace.

I spoke afterwards with Abbot William, telling him of Thomas's death, and what he had said to me concerning Sir Hugh de Warenne. He dismissed it all as idle gossip, and forbade me to mention any of it before my brothers. In these past days he has altered much, indeed I think him grown almost a stranger.

Most days now, Abbot William is with Sir Hugh. They talk in secret, and when they come forth, I see my lord abbot troubled, as though he struggles inwardly with something.

A dreadful thing took place in church today at Nocturns. Brother Precentor had assembled us in the choir for the singing of psalms for the Royal House and the Nocturns of All Saints, when the lord abbot joined us, and with him Sir Hugh de Warenne and Dame Margaret, these last two remaining in the nave.

Abbot William came before us, bidding us remain where we were, and proceeded to speak of the great dying that has crossed all lands and come here within these walls. He said that, unless God could be prevailed upon to act, there was none alive that would escape, neither man nor woman, elder nor child. And it would be as in the days of Noah, except this, that there should be no Ark and no salvation, but that God's punishment should encompass all living. At this, a voice came from the darkness of the choir, asking how God might be prevailed upon that had answered none of our prayers before this.

By answer, Abbot William said that a *clamor* must be set

up before God and in the presence of the people. Few of the brothers had heard of this, for it is an old custom, long out of use, and none in our lifetimes have performed it or seen it performed. Nevertheless, our lord abbot was adamant, and that night, between Nocturns and Matins, he instructed Brother Precentor in the ceremony to be followed, and he in turn explained all to us and prepared us. The rules for the *clamor* and the maledictions that followed had been brought by my lord abbot from France, where they were at one time in common use.

When Matins had been sung, a solemn mass was said, and when the *Paternoster* and *Pax Domini* were done, bread and wine were prepared, as is customary. Whereupon Abbot William instructed the sacrist to cover the pavement before the altar in a coarse cloth, and on this he laid the crucifix, the Gospels, and the holy relics that belong to the abbey church, to lie prostrate there, in a state of humiliation before God. And while he did this, the sacrist closed all doors but one, and barred them with thorns, and placed thorns upon a cross of wood that he laid in the nave, where Sir Hugh de Warenne and his wife were kneeling.

Among the objects that were laid before the altar was one unfamiliar to me. It seemed to be the figure of a man seated upon a chair, his hands raised high in a gesture of supplication. I caught but a brief glimpse of it, but thought it unlike any relic or holy statue I had seen before. I cannot be certain, but it seemed to me that it had ears like a goat's ears, and the head of a ram, and I remembered me of certain things I had been told as a young man concerning Baphomet, the idol of the Saracens.

When all this had been done, we prostrated ourselves on the floor before the altar, singing all the while the words of the psalm, *Ut quid Deus reppulisti in finem.* It was dark all about us, for dawn was still a little while away. As we lay thus prostrate, the custodians rang two bells, continuing until the psalm had reached its end. Whereupon our lord abbot stood alone before the altar, and in a loud voice intoned the *clamor*, which is a prayer beginning with the words, *In spiritu humiliatis,* and to this he added maledictions and curses upon the enemies of God, excommunicating them and damning them for eternity for having caused this pestilence, in that they had provoked God's wrath. But at no time did he name these evildoers, or say in what manner they had provoked God, or for what sins.

When this was done, all candles were put out, leaving us in darkness absolute, and bells were rung, and we remained prostrate upon the floor to sing yet more psalms, capitula, and collects.

That is what I remember of the great *clamor*. But in my heart of hearts I am afraid, for I reckon a terrible wickedness has been done at Thornham Abbey, and that there will be a terrible retribution.

Fourteen

Something happened at Thornham Abbey that should never have happened. The *clamor* – a form of ritual cursing that had been much in vogue in the eleventh and twelfth centuries – seems to have been carried out much in accordance with the correct forms. Yet our anonymous chronicler had the severest misgivings, and I too found myself perturbed by his account.

If the form of malediction used by Abbot William had been, at least, canonical, there could be no question but that the humiliation of relics before the altar had been most irregular. The practice had been prohibited by the Church in the previous century, something William would most certainly have known. As for the supposed reliquary 'in the shape of a little man', I cannot say what it may have been, except that the chronicler was wrong in thinking it a 'Baphomet'. The word is no more than a corruption of the name of the Arab prophet, and since Mohammedans do not worship idols, the notion of statues of a god by this name is simple fiction. All the same, I would be prepared to wager that this strange object was indeed what Sir Hugh de Warenne had brought to Thornham Abbey.

Simone arrived as planned a few days later, accompanied by her parents and Bertrand, the latter fully recovered from his illness, but ill at ease on this, his first trip away from France.

Already unsettled by the move consequent on his father's death, the boy was understandably bewildered to find himself in a foreign country where everyone spoke a strange language. When we were all together, we spoke in French, of course, but in wider company English was needed. I promised Bertrand that I would give him lessons, hoping in this way to secure his affections. I knew little of children, for they had never figured in my life until then; but I prided myself on having some knowledge of sound education, and hoped to win Bertrand to myself as the supervisor of his schooling in years to come.

Both my parents are dead, and I have no close relations apart from my sister Agnes in Trumpington and a brother, Albert, who lives in Edinburgh and visits us here very little. Since our wedding was to be a quiet affair, I had no plans to tour the counties, exhibiting Simone to aunts here and cousins there.

When, however, I explained to Agnes that I had secured lodgings for Simone and her family in a boarding house on Chesterton Road, she lost her temper with me for the first time since we were children, said that she and her husband would never hear of such a thing, and made immediate arrangements to accommodate them at her own home. I cannot say but that I was immensely delighted. It would give Simone a splendid opportunity to get to know Agnes, who would, after all, be her first female friend in the city, at the same time permitting Bertrand to form ties with his cousins-to-be.

Herbert, the elder of Agnes's two children, was, at ten, rather an old playmate for Bertrand, but Alice, my niece, was almost exactly the same age, and of such a sweet temperament that I was sure they would quickly form the closest of attachments. At that age, language is little impediment to friendship, and I was confident that a few weeks in one another's company would soon see Bertrand in possession of more English than I could teach him in months.

Having recovered from the initial shock of hearing that I was to be married after a life of bachelorhood, my sister was cautious as to what manner of wife I might have procured for myself. She has never been overly fond of the French, ever since an unfortunate experience in childhood when she caught sight of her governess *sans* wig, teeth, and corsets. I think she was at first anxious on my behalf, hearing that I was to join myself to a French widow, imagining, I do not doubt, some frumpish dowager, or, even worse, a harridan of advanced years and freakish notions.

Her relief on seeing Simone (though I confess I had well prepared her by tedious description) was palpable, but her instant affection for my fiancée could not be disguised. Even my brother-in-law Charles, a man not given to enthusiasm for anything but a biological specimen, waxed eloquent after dinner that first evening, extolling Simone's eyes, figure, and manner as though she had been his own discovery.

Everyone loved Simone, and I spent my days showing her off to colleagues and friends, bursting with pride and filled with a mounting sense of our coming happiness. Simone was entranced by everything she saw: by the colleges, by the river, by the meadows that led down to Grantchester. The freedom we had enjoyed in the Pyrenées, when she was my guide and I a disinterested scholar, was denied us now we found ourselves in the more strait-laced atmosphere of Cambridge. Propriety, still a fierce watchdog in those days, followed us everywhere, and we seldom had an opportunity to be alone.

A few days after Simone's arrival, Charles and Agnes presented us with the most wonderful surprise. Simone, her parents, and I returned from tea with the Master of my college late one afternoon to find them all but hugging themselves in raptures. When asked the reason, they were at first mysterious, then smug. Finally, Agnes could stand it no longer and blurted out that they had found the perfect place for us to rent right there in Trumpington, a little Georgian house midway between Anstey Hall and the church, and scarcely two minutes' walk from their own.

We went to inspect it first thing in the morning. Simone pronounced it indeed perfect, I agreed (though I think I would at that time have agreed with anything), and we went directly to the agents to sign our lease. Bertrand was quiet, needing time, as I thought, to adjust to the idea of yet another home. But I wonder now. I wonder if he had not sensed something amiss even then.

That same afternoon, Atherton appeared at the Napiers', having been sent on there by my college porter. I must admit that the sight of him as he entered the drawing room, shuffling and nervous, an odd creature out of his depth amidst so much domesticity, struck me as though someone had dashed a jug of ice-cold water in my face. Simone later asked me why I had gone so pale to see him come in, and I lied to her for the first time, regretting that I did so; nonetheless, I was determined she should have no knowledge of the business in which he and I were involved.

He apologised for the interruption in that awkward way he has, and asked if he could speak with me alone. Charles, who knew him slightly on account of their common membership on a couple of university committees, looked at me askance, but nodded permission for us to retire. We went to the study, where lights had already been lit for Charles, who likes to work there undisturbed in the evenings.

"I'm most awfully sorry to intrude like this," Atherton began, "but I had to see you."

"Did you get my note?"

We had not met since the day of our abortive visit to Lethaby. I had sent a note to Sidney Sussex, saying that my researches in Cambridge and Ely had borne some fruit, but without elaborating on what I had discovered about Abbot William. Atherton had not replied.

"Yes," he said, "but that's not why I've come."

I noticed now that his face, dim in the fading daylight of the drawing room, was drawn and pale, and that his eyes were restless.

"Has something happened?" I asked, knowing my question was redundant.

"My mother's grave. That is . . . She was buried with my father at Ely, as you know, and the grave refilled. The mason is to carve her name next week – a space was left expressly for that purpose."

"Words have appeared on the stone?"

He shook his head.

"That would have been preferable," he said. We were seated by now, facing one another in large armchairs. The gas-light dimmed and brightened again above our heads, casting our shadows across the wall. "I had to confirm the details of the inscription with the sacristan," he continued, "so I visited him yesterday at the cathedral. I thought him a little odd at first: he'd been a friendly man on the few occasions I'd met him in the past, but yesterday he seemed rather stiff. We talked for a while, mainly reminiscences of my mother, whom he had known in the days when my father was bishop.

"It was as I was leaving that he admitted to me what was troubling him. He considers it one of his duties to ensure that the cathedral precincts are clear of interlopers at night. Sometimes vagrants go there, and even women of uncertain morals. The sacristan does his rounds about ten o'clock. Last week, while passing through the graveyard with his lantern, he noticed that the flowers had been disturbed on my parents' grave, which lies near the path.

"On reaching the grave, he bent down to straighten the wreaths that had fallen, and, as he did so, he heard . . ." Atherton broke off, agitated. He looked at me appealingly, as though I might be able to help him, but I remained silent, locked in my own dread of what was to come. "He swears to this, you understand, he maintains the truth of it. Not a fanciful man, you see, not prone to . . . fancy. You do understand?"

"Yes," I answered, pitying him, "I understand perfectly. Go on. What did he hear?"

"Sounds coming from beneath the earth. He made quite sure of that. They were not in the vicinity, but from the grave itself."

"I see." I felt darkness growing in me again, after days of sunshine. I pushed all thought of Simone from me and asked him again. "What sort of sounds?"

"Bangings. Short cries, much broken. Scratchings. He thought at first my mother must have been buried alive, and was making haste to summon men to dig when he saw it was impossible. There would not have been air enough for her to survive so long. Not by many days."

"And did he summon anyone?"

"He left the place in horror and has not ventured out by night since. I asked him if he had said anything to the dean, but he said he could not face him or any other member of the chapter with such a story."

"He has returned to your mother, then."

Atherton nodded.

"What can we do?"

I hesitated. I knew what had to be done, and I knew it must be done that night, but the thought of leaving Simone there and going to that churchyard filled me with terror. But I thought of the promise I had made. Tonight would not make an end of the matter, but it might bring Atherton's mother and his brother rest.

"We must go to Ely tonight," I said. "Are you willing?"

I saw the hesitation on his face, and the fear. But he nodded gamely.

"I'll do whatever has to be done," he said.

"You must make up your mind to that," I said. "There may be much to do before the night is over."

Fifteen

It is best, I think, if I pass over in as few words as possible what went forward that night in the churchyard at Ely Cathedral. Much of what Atherton and I did was performed under the cover of darkness, and out of sight of any onlooker, cleric or lay. Apart from a dark lantern, I had brought with me only a box of consecrated wafers and a fifteenth-century liturgical volume, containing certain texts for use in exorcism. These latter I had picked up from my college rooms before heading for the train.

Our task took well over an hour to accomplish, and by the time it ended we were barely able to return to Cambridge by the last train. Atherton seemed drained, almost on the edge of a nervous collapse, for the grave had not been quiet when we first arrived, and he said he could still hear terrible sounds ringing in his head. I too found it impossible wholly to rid myself of them.

That night I was in no state to return to Trumpington, nor was I composed enough to see Simone again until the following evening. In the morning, I sent one of the college servants to present the excuse that an emergency had arisen concerning one of my students. When I saw the family before dinner that evening, I reiterated my apologies, but I could see that my precipitate departure the day before had awakened some measure of disquiet.

Simone and I found an opportunity after dinner to walk for a while in the garden unchaperoned. The darkness, for all it was filled with her gentle presence, reminded me uneasily of the night before, and brought back a host of unpleasant memories.

"You are very quiet, Richard," she said after we had walked a little way. There was a scent of woodsmoke in the air. The first leaves had started to fall.

"I'm sorry, my love," I replied. "I'm a little preoccupied."

"Not on account of me, I hope." I could detect a tiny edge of anxiety in her voice, and hastened to reassure her.

"Good heavens, no. How could you think such a thing?"

"You don't seem yourself. As if . . . It is as if a cloud has come over you." She paused while we walked a little further, arm in arm. I wanted to stop and kiss her, hold her hard against me as a shield to ward off the darkness, but in that mood I could not trust myself. She must know nothing of what had happened, what might yet take place.

"You have changed since Mr Atherton's arrival," she went on. "Charles wonders how you come to know him."

"Oh, Matthew and I are old friends," I lied. "Charles moves in quite different circles. He would not know of our acquaintance."

"He appeared distressed when he came here yesterday."

"Yes, he was disturbed about something. A private matter. I really can't tell you more without breaking a confidence."

"A woman, perhaps?"

Above us, tall trees stood dark against the sky, their branches vaguely threatening. I shook my head.

"No," I replied. "He has had some personal tragedies this year. His brother died in January, his mother but a few weeks ago. He has not yet got over her death."

"I see. Yes, I must have misjudged him."

We turned to more personal matters, and by the end of the walk Matthew Atherton and his visit had been forgotten.

That night, before I returned to college, Charles himself took me aside to ask me about Atherton. He was rather awkward, as though preparing himself for a difficult interview with a student in danger of being sent down. In spite of our relationship, Charles and I were not close friends. For one thing, he was somewhat pious, a regular attender both at college chapel and his parish church, and inclined to fudge the contradictions between his science and his faith. He was also rather stuffy in matters of social convention, a tendency he had inherited from his father, who had been a professor of theology noted for his traditionalist views.

"I'm sorry to ask about this, Richard, but I feel a certain . . . obligation."

"Is it about Simone?"

"Gracious, no. We're all delighted with Simone. Couldn't be more so. And her parents are perfectly acceptable. A schoolteacher is not a don, of course, but he seems most erudite and . . ."

"Please get to the point, Charles."

We were in the study. The weight of his books on all sides lay on me like a strap. I wanted to go outside again, to breathe fresh air scented with woodsmoke. Among the books, shadows seemed to crawl like lobsters.

"Yes, of course. The thing is, I couldn't help wondering how you came to know Atherton. I shouldn't have thought him your type."

"My type? What's wrong with him?"

"Well, surely you know his reputation. Some of the men

in my college think him odd. His father was a bishop, and I believe a brother was rector of a parish somewhere or other, but he himself is known to have unorthodox opinions."

"In that case, Charles, why on earth should you be surprised to find I know him? You've expressed disapproval of my opinions often enough."

"Oh, you're merely a freethinker. There are enough of your sort in the university, that's hardly important. But Atherton's different again. He doesn't scoff, but he makes it clear he holds views that other people might find . . . disturbing."

"Such as?"

"I believe he disregards more than religion, Richard. There are some who say he considers himself above common morality, that he holds all ethical and moral systems to be mere conveniences. Surely you know this?"

I shook my head. Atherton's private opinions had never been a consideration of mine.

"I have never spoken with him about such matters. My dealings with him have been . . . more academic in nature. I find him a pleasant enough man."

"I only ask you to be careful, Richard. You have a reputation to protect. And, if I may dare say so, you will very shortly have the reputations of a wife and child as well. Take care with Atherton. Break with him if you can. If not, be sure your dealings with him remain, as you say, academic."

We parted after that, and I returned to college, revolving in my mind how Atherton had offended Charles and his set. There was no question of my breaking with him. The promise I had made to his mother still had force over me, more than ever since the night before.

Simone and her father visited me the next day in my rooms,

where I had just finished a tutorial. The wedding was fast approaching, and we still had preparations to make. My skip, Bott brought tea, and as we sat in front of the fire eating buttered muffins, we could hear the muffled voices of the college choir, as they practised in the chapel nearby.

When we had eaten, I showed René some books I had mentioned during my stay in France. There was one particularly heavy volume which I had acquired earlier that year from Mr Quaritch, and this I had to transfer to the table. We spent a little time leafing through the text, René entranced to have seen at last a series of engravings of which he had until then only heard the reputation.

As I closed the book and made to lift it from the table, René noticed a map that I had spread out there some hours earlier. This was a plan of Thornham Abbey, drawn by Bradwell in the course of his excavations. I had been going through it in order to familiarise myself with the layout of the site, preparatory to making a visit there in the next few days. To peruse the plan was to make vivid once more the details of the anonymous account I had read. Here were the infirmaries, one for the canons, one for the lay brothers, here the abbot's lodging, where William had entertained Sir Hugh de Warenne and his wife, here was the abbey church, the choir, the altar at the east end before which William had deposited his relics and performed his ritual of *magnus clamor*, invoking God knows what forces in a vain attempt to save his people from the plague. Or had it been to save himself and his noble guests alone?

René has a fondness for maps and plans. He will often pore over one for hours, extracting from it all he needs to know about a place. Bradwell's delightful plan, so minutely executed and so lovingly adorned with sketches of the ruins, drew his attention at once. It had been inadvertent of me, I should have preferred to say nothing about Thornham.

"Such a beautiful plan, Richard. So full of detail." He glanced at the title in the right-hand corner. "Yes, of course, I have heard of Thornham Abbey. A great Benedictine establishment. A daughter-house of Fleury, through Abingdon, am I not right? Simon of Malmesbury wrote his *Anecdota* there, yes?"

I nodded glumly. I had no wish to excite his further interest.

"You have been there recently?"

I shook my head. "I was thinking of going in the new year, or perhaps the spring."

"But surely it is not far from here. I would so much like to visit the place. All these colleges of yours are very well, but I wish to see some ruins, I wish to breathe some of your fine country air. I would like very much to visit Thornham Abbey. And I am sure my dear Simone would love to go there too. We shall make a picnic."

Before I could protest, Simone was beside me, urging me to agree.

"A day in the country will be wonderful," she said. "Papa can visit his ancient monuments, my mother can bake tarts with your sister for us to bring, Bertrand can play in the fields with Herbert and Alice, and you and I can have a long walk and talk about what we will do when we are married."

I could not refuse her. How could I have looked into those eyes, so full of love and passion, and refused? She enchanted me, and what she wished, I performed. Good God, I feel it tearing at me even as I write, the regret that I have lived with since, the remorse that has eaten away all the years between.

I should have known that evil knows no boundaries, and that it has no pity.

"Yes," I whispered, and I caressed her face as I did so, "we shall all go to Thornham Abbey."

Sixteen

The morning of the picnic was vibrant with autumn sunshine. There was a nip in the air, and a promise of colder weather to follow, but the whole world that morning seemed fresh and energising, and we set out in the best of spirits: Simone, her parents, Bertrand, Agnes, Herbert, Alice and myself. Charles absented himself, pleading a light cold; I suspected him of malingering, for I knew he did not feel it entirely proper to go on outings on a Sunday. We left early, and were at Ely by ten, where we hired an open carriage from a man called Sudley.

I put on a brave face, and managed to convince the others that I could think of nothing more delightful than a trip to Thornham Abbey. I had done my best to dismiss the fears that had first arisen when the idea of the outing was put forward. Danger lay, not in Thornham, but at Thornham St Stephen. That was where William de Lindesey's remains lay buried, that was where he had been released from his long imprisonment. Yet I could not wholly cast aside the thought that it had been at the abbey, not the church, that he had first invoked the evil that had in time engulfed him.

But that day, that slightly chilly day at the end of autumn, no one but I had any thought of evil. The children were delirious at the thought of eating in the open air, the adults enamoured with the place or the weather or each other. On this, our first day away from the constraints of formal society, I truly think Simone and I became lovers for the first time. There is great irony in that, as I think back, and yet a certain logic too, quite inexorable, as though the conjunction of love and evil had been travelling towards us for a long time.

The minutes that Simone and I snatched for ourselves apart from the others were spent for each other wholly, without reserve. We walked hand in hand through Thornham Wood, among shadows, and at the same moment paused, and kissed, and did not separate for a very long time. And then we heard the children's voices coming in the distance, and the spell was broken. As we left the woods, all we desired was to be married without delay.

René had insisted on bringing Bradwell's plan with him, and, while the women and children busied themselves in preparations for lunch, he pressed me to accompany him on a tour of the site.

Though much overgrown by grass, weeds, and ivy, Thornham Abbey is still quite well preserved. Parts of the west front and almost the entire presbytery remain standing, the chapter house gate is virtually intact, there are five cloister arches still in place, and parts of other walls. It is surprisingly easy, with the help of a good plan, to form a coherent impression of the whole establishment as it had been on the eve of its dissolution.

As we passed from ruin to ruin, tracing the lines of one building after another, my earlier mood of elation gave way to one of introspection. At one point, as we stood in what had been the church's east end, René identified the spot where the altar had once stood. A flat rectangular stone still lay there, on which the altar must have rested.

I stood there, looking back westwards along the chancel,

tracing with my eye the stones that marked the choir, imagining it in darkness, as it had been on the night of the *clamor*, and almost, if I closed my eyes, I could hear the voices of the monks chanting their prayers in plainsong, and the silence following, and the voice of Abbot William, those soft, arrogant tones that I had heard less than a year before.

"Are you feeling all right, Richard?"

René was beside me, a look of concern on his face. He had seen me totter and almost fall. I took his arm to steady myself.

"Yes, yes," I said, "I'm fine. I just felt a little dizzy, that's all."

"It's time for lunch. You will be dizzy if you do not eat. Let's go and see if the food is ready."

We had our picnic in the area marked by Bradwell as the refectory. There were Scotch eggs and cheese and pâté (brought from France), quails' eggs, slices of ham and chicken, little game pies from Sewell the butcher, and cake. Mme Seillière had baked fresh bread the night before, light French loaves quite unlike our stodgy local fare, and René had presented us with three bottles of wine, that he had brought for just such an occasion. The children had pop, and ate more cake than anything.

I scarcely ate, though I did my best to conceal the fact. Simone noticed, and expressed concern that I might be ill. I made light of it, saying I was too much keyed up about the coming wedding to have a proper appetite. She believed me, and apologised for eating as heartily as ever.

After lunch, Simone asked to be taken round the abbey. Agnes watched the children, who had returned to play, while René and Mme Seillière took a ramble beside the little stream that bisected the site. We set off hand in hand, Simone posing questions, I explaining as best I could the significance of the different parts of the ruin.

To most people, ruins are merely romantic or picturesque. But for those of us who visit them with an informed eye, they can be reinhabited and made to live again. And that, I believe, was my undoing, for the more vividly I conjured up for Simone the uses to which the various parts of the abbey had been put, the clearer they became in my own mind's eye.

At one point, we entered the long space that had been the lay infirmary. I was reminded of the scenes that had taken place here during the Black Death, and I began to describe some of this to Simone, in the hope that it would bring the place alive for her. I seemed to have succeeded, for when I finished she was very quiet for a while, as though moved by my account of the unendurable sufferings so many had undergone.

Dark clouds had come up from the east, threatening rain. We sat together on a stump of wall, all curiosity quenched. I thought I might hear, if I listened very hard, the groans of the dying, or the gentle voices of those who ministered to them. And other voices, perhaps, whispering among the stones like memories.

Simone turned to me. Her face had grown pale, or was it just the faltering of the light?

"I thought at first this was a good place," she said. "Quiet, inhabited by the spirits of holy men. Now, I'm not so sure. Something is wrong here, isn't it, Richard? Something is not right."

I said nothing. I looked about me, at the ivy, dark against the grey stone, at the moss, growing across old paving stones and clumped on pillars, at the woods beyond all this, full of shadows, the branches of the trees shedding their leaves in anticipation of winter.

Silently, I put my arm round her shoulders. She shivered involuntarily. It was growing darker, and the breeze was like ice.

"It's time to go," I said. "We'll fetch your parents."

We stood, my hand still in hers, helping her. Beneath our feet, the grass was damp and cold. From the woods where we had been earlier, a clamour of rooks started, black against the deeper blackness of the sky. Simone shivered.

"Someone's watching us," she said.

I looked round, but there was no one. The ruins were empty.

"I can feel it," she said, shivering again. A breeze took her hair and lifted it across her startled face. There were too many shadows here, I thought. Too many shadows, too many eyes.

"Let's go home," I said.

I kept her hand in mine until we were far away from Thornham, and the high octagon of Ely Cathedral had come in sight.

Seventeen

S imone and I were married six days later, on a day of trembling, rose madder light. As we had planned, the ceremony was unpretentious, and the festivities that followed plain. My brother came down from Edinburgh (he is older than I, and was agog to see at first hand the woman who had ensnared me after so many years of dogged bachelorhood), together with a couple of essential aunts and uncles from the shires, the sort who dangle substantial inheritances as bait for impoverished dons such as myself.

A few university friends were also invited, but Matthew Atherton was not among them. I could not have borne the sight of him that day.

As I entered the church, I had the oddest sensation that a scrap of rag or a sheet of dark paper had attached itself to my foot and could not be shaken free. And then, as I started to bend in order to disencumber myself of it, I saw that it had been merely a shadow lying athwart the church door. Moments later, I forgot it entirely as I came to the altar and turned to see Simone arriving on her father's arm, her head bound with fresh autumn flowers, and her unveiled face as I had always known it would be.

Our honeymoon lasted a week. We went to the Lakes, to a cottage owned by James Spalding, my best man. He is the Max

127

Brandt Professor of German, and his 'rustic cottage' turned out to be a most romantic chalet in the Swiss style, hard by the shores of Ullswater. Its steep roofs and large windows do not seem at all out of place there.

There was steady rain for three days, then, on the fourth morning, we awoke to see sunshine streaming across the hills and sparkling on the water, transforming our grey world into paradise.

There were plenty of places for us to walk, hills to climb, sights to see, but we were more than content to remain before the fire in our cottage, with nothing to occupy us but one other. We would talk for hours, almost breathlessly at times. In spite of our talks during those long rambles in the Pyrenées, we still knew next to nothing about each other. It astonished me to find how little a thing my life seemed beside Simone's, for all that I had lived almost twice as long and, as I had thought, richly.

The fact is, I had lived no life at all till then. I had gone from public school to university, from graduation to a college fellowship, and, in time, to a professorship. My friends were dons like myself, bibliophiles, librarians, palaeographers – the chartered accountants of the mind. Most of them were unmarried, as was still common in the university then. My haunts were those of the bachelor, my interests almost entirely antiquarian. Almost all my knowledge of the world had come from books.

At the age of twenty-six, Simone had been married, had given birth to a child, and had been once widowed. It worried me that, having married someone so much older than herself, she might face widowhood again in not many years, and a long life alone.

"Nonsense," she laughed. "You'll live till you're ninety. Till one hundred! There won't seem such a gap between us then.

Who knows? None of us can tell what may happen. I might die before you . . ."

I cut her short, pressing sudden fingers against her lips.

"Don't," I whispered. "You're young, and I couldn't bear to live without you."

Her face grew serious.

"You would learn to live alone again," she said. "I had to learn, and I had never been alone before. Marcellin was twenty-seven when he died. I did not think to lose him. I thought we would live for ever, and never grow old."

She had spoken little of her husband before that, and I had never pressed her to do so. He had been a veterinary surgeon, not long graduated from the school at Lyons. A dog belonging to a neighbour had developed rabies, and Marcellin, trying to rescue its puppies, had been bitten. He had died a few weeks later in terrible agony. Simone had stayed with him to the end. Other than that, she would not speak of his death.

"He was a kind man," she said. "He would never willingly cause an animal pain, unless to cure it. The farmers would have him operate without ether, but he always refused, even if he had to bear the expense himself. The beasts knew he cared for them. They were often quiet when he appeared, even the wildest of them."

"Was he good-looking?"

I had no image in my mind of my predecessor. Perhaps Simone had a photograph somewhere, perhaps she took it out to look at sometimes; but she had not shown it to me.

"Yes," she said, "very handsome. And his body was lean and hard. He was a good husband to me, and a good lover. Why should you care?"

I stroked her hair. I wondered if she was mocking me.

129

"I do care," I said. "I'm jealous of your Marcellin. Of his good looks, of his lean body."

"You have no reason to be jealous. I loved him when he was alive. Now he is dead, and God has sent you to me, and I love you. It is not the same. I would not want it to be the same. It is the difference in you that makes me happy. I love you now, not Marcellin."

"You believe God sent me to you?"

She nodded, very simple in her faith.

"I know you don't believe," she said. "But you will see. God will show you."

"And this God of yours – did He cause Marcellin to die?"

It was a careless question, and I regretted it the moment it had left my mouth. Simone looked at me wide-eyed. She seemed like a child to me, an old child who knows much beyond her years.

"God causes no one to die. An infection kills us, or an accident, or old age."

"Then God is not necessary at all?"

She shook her head slowly.

"That is why He is necessary. Does it not frighten you to live alone in a world where anything may happen? Where a rock falls and crushes you to death? Or a plague wipes out your entire village and leaves you without wife or child or neighbour? God will not stop those things happening, if they are in His will. But we can pray to Him, and if He wills He will protect us from them."

I did not answer. It was not that I did not have replies to all of these explanations, but rather that I had no answer for Simone. She was not a colleague with whom I might fence over the dinner table, but the woman I loved; and at that moment I understood that I could not love her without also loving her belief, however antipathetical it was to my own.

Was that, I wondered, what had happened to Abbot William? Had he despaired of protection from the plague, had he come to believe the world was no longer in the hands of a loving Creator? If so, to what had he turned in his desolation?

We talked no more of death that night. Simone spoke to me about Bertrand, his likes and dislikes, his enjoyments and terrors. He had been badly affected by his father's death, and for months afterwards she had spent most nights watching over him, for he would wake out of a troubled sleep, shouting and afraid. Even now, he would not sleep without a light beside his bed.

She told me Bertrand had a fine singing voice.

"When we lived at St Bertrand," she said, "he was admitted to the choir of the Cathédrale Sainte-Marie. He had already started singing when his father died. I think he would like to have continued, but you have no cathedral in Cambridge."

"The nearest is Ely," I said. "But some of the college chapels have choirs. The best is King's. We could apply for a place in the choir school."

She fell in with my suggestion at once, and we began to talk, as we did so often that week, of the future. Her ambition was that Bertrand should become fluent in English, that he should excel at school, and that, in due course, he should take a degree at the university. By the time we had finished, we had all but lived an entire life for the boy, without his consent. But, in truth, all either of us wanted was that he should be happy.

It is quiet almost beyond imagining in that stretch of the Lakes, far from any town, a mile or more from the nearest neighbour.

The only sounds at night are those of waves lapping the shore, and night-birds, and sometimes, far away, the barking of a sheepdog or a fox. That night we went to bed late. I had still not grown accustomed to sharing my bed with someone else, and that night I did not fall asleep easily. I remember thinking a great deal about Marcellin and the manner of his death, and I know I dwelt for a long time on my own inadequacies. It seemed impossible to me that I should ever make a good husband to Simone or a wise father to Bertrand, for I felt I must fall far short of Marcellin in all respects.

In spite of this, I fell asleep at last, and the silence must have soothed me, for I did not awake until shortly before dawn. At first, I noticed nothing amiss. It was only when I reached out my hand to touch Simone that I realised she was no longer in bed beside me. Nor was she in our bedroom.

I rose and slipped on my dressing-gown. It was very cold. I do not know why, but my heart was beating. I felt a sense of dread, as though something sinister had happened or was about to happen. There was a lamp beside the bed. I lit it and went out into the corridor.

Simone was downstairs in the sitting room. A candle was burning near her, which she must have lit to assist her down the stairs. She was standing by the large window that looks out onto the lake. Hearing my step behind her, she started. I could not see her clearly in that low light, but as she turned I caught a glimpse of her face, more drawn and pale than I had seen it.

"Is something wrong, dear?" I asked.

She crossed the room to me and came into my arms, and as I took her to myself, I noticed she was trembling.

"You'll catch your death of cold," I said. She was wearing only her night-dress.

"I'm all right," she said. "I was about to go back to bed anyway."

"I asked if anything was wrong."

She hesitated.

"I thought I heard something outside. It must have woken me. Footsteps, perhaps. Something scraping on the rocks. I'm not sure. I got up and came down here to have a look without disturbing you."

"Far better to have woken me."

"You were fast asleep. It didn't matter. I'm not afraid of the dark."

"Did you see anything?"

She hesitated again.

"I'm not sure," she said. "It's still quite dark outside. There was something. No more than a shadow, very low to the ground, crawling quite slowly. It went along the edge of the lake. It might have been a man, I can't be sure."

I went to the window and looked out. Pale light had appeared in the east, and was already touching the surface of the lake with tiny flecks of gold. I cast my eye along the rocks and sandbars of the shore, but I could see nothing. All the time, I felt sick at heart, but I could say nothing to Simone.

I turned to see her standing behind me with her candle in one hand. Her hair tumbled about her shoulders, catching fragments of the flame.

"Let's go back to bed," I said.

Later that morning, we went outside and scoured the lakeside for signs of an intruder. The little boat that was tied up at our landing stage had not been tampered with, and we could find no footprints anywhere. I began to think that perhaps our night visitor had been a fox or a badger after all. But as we were heading back to the chalet, Simone stooped down and picked up something from the grass beneath the sitting room window. It was a scrap of black rag, coarsely woven and torn at one end, as though ripped from a larger piece. She held it in her hands for a few moments, then raised it to her nose and smelled it, only to throw it from her in disgust.

I glanced down to where it lay, black against the grass, almost reproaching Simone's fastidiousness. Carefully, I picked it up again. Once we were inside, I threw it on the fire, watching until it had been wholly consumed.

Eighteen

We got back to Cambridge late on Sunday evening. Simone's parents, Agnes, Charles, and the three children were waiting for us at the station. There was a fly to take us newly-weds directly to Trumpington, while the others followed in two separate carriages.

Agnes and Seillière (aided, I need scarcely say, by a bevy of maids borrowed from friends) had, in our absence, turned our rented house into something approximating everyone's idea of a genteel family home. Agnes had even introduced some furniture that had belonged to our parents, to lend the house what she called a 'homely air'.

"You will, of course, want your own furniture as soon as it can be arranged," Agnes hectored me gently as we went in. "But the rented furniture is of reasonable quality, and I am sure it will do very well for a month or two, until you are both settled."

As I remember it, the rest of that evening was spent in exhortation, advice and instruction. Treating Simone quite as if she were a new bride of seventeen, and not a widow entered upon her second marriage, my sister and her mother together undertook my wife's initiation into the arcane mysteries of running a middle-class home on the outskirts of Cambridge. I think Agnes feared that Simone would otherwise introduce

French ways into her household, and that before long our home would become an occasion of scandal for the neighbourhood. Albertine Seillière, conversely, seemed to have been quite concerned to prevent her daughter being sucked too precipitately into English ways.

We menfolk stayed clear of all this to-ing and fro-ing by remaining like folk under siege in the very fine room that I had designated my library and which, while I had been in the Lakes, my dear René had furnished with those of my books that had already been marked for removal to my home. I still planned to keep my college rooms for tutorials or small gatherings of friends after Hall or chapel after evensong.

Charles left early in order to ensure that Alice and Herbert were in bed by nine. Herbert attended St Faith's (which we all referred to as 'Goody's'), while young Alice had recently started at the Perse School for Girls. That was Agnes's idea, for Charles quite disapproved of girls having an education at all. I told him of our plan to send Bertrand to the choir school at King's.

"A first-rate idea. He can sing Dufay for them in the original. They'd like that. None of them can sing French, or Italian for that matter. They make a stab at Latin, but the Catholics do it much better. Young Herbert can't sing. Never could. None of us Napiers ever had much of a voice."

He departed on this note, but as he got to the front gate, he turned and came back to me, leaving Alice and Herbert waiting.

"I forgot to mention, your friend Atherton turned up last week. Said he was looking for you. Didn't seem to know you were on your honeymoon. I thought he was a friend of yours."

"An acquaintance, Charles. I told you."

"Yes, well, he said he needed to talk to you. He was taken aback by the honeymoon – seemed to think you weren't planning on getting married for some time yet. I put him right. He wanted me to pass the message on when you got back. Now I've done it."

I thanked him and went back inside. However hard I struggled, it seemed I could not escape the toils into which Matthew Atherton had led me.

Albertine had prepared a light supper for us all. Agnes went off home to dine with Charles. Bertrand ate with us. This would be his first night under our roof, our first night together as a family. He was silent throughout the meal, estimating, no doubt, the features of the new world into which he had been brought, unconsulted and largely unprepared. Simone sat beside him, smiling at him often, and from time to time stroking his head, as though to soothe him.

When we had eaten, Simone took Bertrand upstairs, sticking firmly to the bedtime rituals they had developed in their years together at St Bertrand-de-Comminges. She came down after about fifteen minutes.

"Darling," she said to me, "his father always went up to him last, to kiss him good-night. Do you think . . . ?"

I nodded agreement and hastily made my way upstairs. Not unnaturally, I was a little in awe of this new role I was to play, and nervous of my presumption in stepping so boldly into another man's shoes.

Bertrand was awake. His night-light burned steadily on the bedside table. In his arms he embraced a toy rabbit he had brought from France. He seemed much younger than seven, a little boy snatched from all that was familiar, cradling his last tangible link with home.

"I've come to say good-night, Bertrand."

I spoke in French, for it was the language we had come to use between us. In time, I thought, we must change to English; but not yet. He did not answer. When I drew closer, he turned his face away, and I noticed that his eyes were brimming with tears.

I almost went back for Simone. She would know what to do and what to say, I thought. I felt helpless, knowing nothing of children or their comfort. But I reckoned it would be cowardly of me to sneak away like that and find someone else to do my dirty work. I sat down on the edge of the bed.

"What's wrong, old man?" I asked. My own father had called me 'old man', and I supposed it would do well enough under the circumstances, even in French.

He did not answer me at once, and for a while I did not think he would answer at all, and was at a loss as to how I might ever extract a reply from him. In the end, I did not have to. The words were there, all he had to do was find his way to them.

"I want my father back," he said.

It came to me like a shiver of desperation how little use I was in this brave new world into which I had so rashly entered.

"Your father? I . . . Surely, Bertrand, surely you know your beloved father is dead."

"He's not dead. He can't be. It's a lie."

He turned his eyes on mine. Fierce eyes that burned me with their heat.

"I wish it were a lie," I said. "But it is the terrible truth. Surely your mother has told you that. She would not lie about such a thing. She misses him terribly as well. I know she does."

"I don't care. I don't care if it is true. I still want him back."

It was on my tongue to cry, "the dead do not return", but I swallowed the words, knowing their untruth.

"I am to be your new father, Bertrand," was all I said instead. They were the hardest words I have ever spoken. It seemed so presumptuous in me to imagine I might take another man's place.

"You can't be my father. *Jamais, jamais, jamais.*"

"Nevertheless, I shall try," I said. His desperation upset me very much. I was ill-equipped to deal with it. "And you must try to help me. I love your mother very much, and I want to love you as well. But I cannot do it without your help."

He was silent at this talk of love, for he was, in truth, not ready for it yet.

Perhaps I should have bent down to kiss him, or offered to tell him a story; but I sensed it was too early for such affection. I rose instead and went to the door. As I put my hand to it, he called me back.

"Mother says I am to be sent away to a big school." His voice was choked with emotion, and I could see that this was the core of his anxiety.

I shook my head.

"You're not to be sent away. The school will take you as a day-boy, and you'll live here as normal with your mother and myself. And it's not at all a big school. Quite the opposite. The boys are choristers at King's College. It's a small chapel, not even as large as the cathedral where you sang before. Your mother says you have a fine voice."

He shrugged.

"I'd like to hear you sing some time," I said. "Perhaps some evening after dinner?"

"I don't like to sing on my own. It's better in a choir. No one notices you too much."

"I'm sure that's true," I smiled. "But I would like to hear you all the same."

"Do you sing?"

"No, I have no voice. But I play the pianoforte tolerably well. I could play for you if you like. And teach you some English songs. Not the sort of thing you sing in church. Jolly things. 'Green Grow the Rushes'. That sort of thing."

He asked me to sing it for him, and I did, in a rather hushed voice. Some accompaniment might have helped, but he seemed to like it well enough. I explained some of the words for him, but I must confess I had as little idea as he had what they really meant.

This time, as I was leaving, he stopped me with a different question.

"Who is William?" he asked.

He did not use the name 'William', of course, but 'Guillaume'. It took a moment for me to see what he meant, and a moment longer for the truth to dawn on me.

"I don't understand," I said. My mouth was dry with fear. "I know no one of that name. Did he say his name was 'William'?"

Bertrand shook his head.

"He spoke to me in French. But he said you knew him."

"When . . . When was this?"

"While you were away. The day after the wedding. I was in the garden, playing with Herbert and Alice. The game they call 'Hide and Seek'. A man came up to me and asked where he might find you. I told him you had gone away, that you had gone on a 'honeymoon'. He seemed surprised, then asked me where you had gone. I told him the name of the place, of the lake you had gone to. I asked him who he was, and he said his name was 'Guillaume', and that

140

you would know who he was. Then he thanked me and went away."

"What was he like, can you remember?"

"An old man. His hair was white. He was . . . dressed like a priest."

"And have you seen him since then?"

He shook his head.

"Not since then. I'm sorry, I should have told you before. But I forgot. I didn't like to think about him much."

"Why was that?"

He shook his head, reluctant to say more.

"Please, Bertrand – why didn't you want to think about this man?"

"I . . . I don't know. Perhaps . . . I think he frightened me a little."

"How was that?"

"He . . . When he came behind me, he was so quiet I didn't know anyone was there. I thought . . ." He hesitated. I could sense the fear in his eyes.

"It's all right, Bertrand, you can tell me."

"I thought . . . For a moment, I thought he was a ghost."

Nineteen

René and Albertine left as planned. Everyone was in floods of tears throughout the day of their departure. In the few weeks they had been with us, they had won the affections of the entire family, and the warm regard of many of our friends. Their departure was preceded by a farewell breakfast at our new home in Trumpington.

It had been agreed that Charles alone should accompany my parents-in-law on the first leg of their journey, to see them safely through London and on to the boat train at Waterloo. Simone and I had very much wanted to go, but Albertine had set herself vehemently against it. Bertrand, she said, had endured too much upheaval for the present. His grandparents' departure would itself upset him greatly, and should Simone and I also leave, albeit briefly, it would be bound to add considerably to his misery and make it harder for him to settle with us.

Once they had gone, we dedicated ourselves to creating an air of normality in our home. For several weeks now, our lives had worn an air of unseasonable holiday. My teaching duties had been fitted in amidst a hectic round of visits, receptions, and outings. I had neglected my students and lost valuable time in the preparation of my manuscript. Now all that had to change. I would spend more time at college, Bertrand would start school, and Simone would learn to be mistress of a modest English family.

Our household consisted, apart from ourselves, of a maid, Mary, a cook and housekeeper, Mrs Lumley, and a boy of fourteen to fetch and carry, Ned Larkin. They had all three been carefully selected by Agnes, following assiduous enquiries among the widest possible range of female acquaintances, informed shopkeepers, prim governesses, old maids, laundresses, and, for all I know, tramps and roadsweepers. We found ourselves well content with them.

Simone had had no staff at home in St Bertrand, and to begin with found the task of ordering others to carry out simple household tasks quite uncongenial. There was, too, much occasion for misunderstanding, given that her mastery of English was still limited, and that the accents of our trusty servants were broad enough to tax the comprehension of even the most experienced resident of the county.

They all lived in. Mary and Mrs Lumley had small rooms in the attic, while Ned made do with a warm space on the kitchen floor. We paid them what Agnes insisted was the 'going rate', though I rather think Simone thought it niggardly and added small *douceurs* from time to time. The women had one day off a week, and we were careful to make no demands on them after eleven o'clock at night. On Wednesdays, when Mrs Lumley had a day to herself, I had food sent up from college. Charles and Agnes did not altogether approve of that, but I considered it fair, and would not be dissuaded from it.

The day following René and Albertine's departure, Simone and I took Bertrand to the new school-house on Grange Road, where he was auditioned for the King's College choir. The headmaster and choirmaster together conducted us to the practice room, where they spent a little time chatting with

Bertrand, in the most atrocious French, in an effort to put him at his ease. Our presence was permitted throughout the proceedings as being conducive to the boy's composure.

They gave him a piece to sing at last, a traditional French carol, '*Quelle est cette odeur agréable?*'. It was not a piece I knew, but it was beautiful, and poignant, and I shivered inwardly as I listened to him, to the purity and gravity of that fragile voice.

> *Quelle est cette odeur agréable,*
> *Bergers, qui ravit tous nos sens?*
> *S'exhale-t-il rien de semblable*
> *Au milieu des fleurs du printemps?*

He sang as if without effort, and when he finished there was silence for a time, and for a little time after that. The choirmaster looked at the headmaster, and there were no words between them, but I knew they had heard what I had heard.

Bertrand had mentioned that at the Cathédrale Sainte-Marie they had chants according to melodies recorded some twenty years ago by Dom Prosper Guéranger, a monk who had refounded the monastery of Saint-Pierre de Solesmes. He had brought with him the music for a part of the Ordinary of the mass, *Kyrie, fons bonitatis, pater ingenite, a quo bona cuncta procedunt, eleison,* and this, at their request, he now sang in a solemn voice, lingering in long melismae on single syllables, drawing them out in note after note until it seemed each word might last an eternity. And we sat and listened as though an angel had come to the room.

I can hear him still if I close my eyes, his voice is inside me like no other voice. If all else were to be stripped away from me, leaving me naked to my soul, Bertrand's voice would still remain, full of grace, and moving me to tears.

They did not ask him to sing again. There was no question of turning him away. For a voice like his, they would have sold the rest of the choir to the first college to ask for them. We were quietly happy as we took him home. He was silent, still unsure of himself, still awed by the school and the masters he had met after the practice. His one comfort had been the French master, a little apelike man from Lyons, M. Aristide.

That night we attended choral evensong at King's. Bertrand, accustomed to the formalities of a Catholic mass, was bemused by the proceedings, but impressed by the high quality of the singing. The chapel itself, its ceiling trembling high above our heads in candlelight, was later pronounced by him to be the most beautiful place he had ever seen, but he did not understand why there were no statues and, above all, no images of Our Lady, for whom he had a child's devotion. My attempts to explain the origins of our national Church were, I fear, met with incomprehension.

It had been agreed between us that Simone and Bertrand should continue to worship at the Catholic church where we had been married. The priest there, Father Cahill, was a pleasant Irish man who had no objections to Bertrand's singing in an Anglican choir, but insisted on his regular appearance at mass. Bertrand had been confirmed a few months before his father's death, and was, so Simone told me, assiduous in attending confession.

It had grown dark by the time we left the chapel. As we did so, I noticed a figure detach itself from the shadows of the Gibbs Building and step towards me. It was Matthew Atherton, and he looked quite ill, much changed from when I had last seen him. He came out from the shadows, as I say, and grasped my hand, and drew me tight towards him, away from Simone and Bertrand.

"Asquith," he breathed in a harsh voice. He sounded unfamiliar to me, as though he were a stranger. "I've got to speak to you."

"What's all this about?" I glanced round, catching sight of Simone. She stood a few feet away, watching us anxiously, alarmed by this precipitate appearance of a man I had told her I scarcely knew.

"I've been trying to find you for days," he rushed on, breathless, almost hoarse. I could not see him well, for he had pulled me back among the shadows. His face seemed pale, and I noticed a heavy trace of alcohol on his breath. "You've not been in your college rooms, and every time I've tried your sister's they've told me you're away, you're not to be disturbed. Then I thought of asking the porter here. He gave me your new address. Your housekeeper said I'd find you here."

"What is it, man? What's wrong?"

"Wrong? I wonder you need to ask." His hand was still on my arm, clutching it tightly. I could tell he was in the grip of powerful emotions, and I dreaded what he might reveal.

"The shadows," he said. "What else? Every night now. Sometimes during the day. On the wall, on the floor, always when you least expect them, and then scuttling away when you look at them directly. Sometimes I almost think it's just a single shadow, that it's always the same shadow returning. You've seen it too, haven't you, you and your precious little wife? Admit it, why can't you?"

I tried in vain to calm him, but the more he spoke, the more agitated he became. I was frightened for Bertrand, who must be disturbed by this strange man accosting me.

"Look here," I said, feeling all the time a sickness in the pit of my stomach that I dared not admit to. "This is no good. I can't make sense of what you're saying. Try to get a hold of yourself, and I'll take you back to your college. You can tell me everything there. But first, I've got to get my wife and stepson back to Trumpington."

I don't know how I managed to shake him off, but after a short tussle I rejoined my family.

"It's Atherton," I said. "He's very upset about something, I'm not sure what."

"He seems drunk," said Simone. "Is that true? Is he drunk?"

I nodded.

"Yes," I said, "he is a little. But more upset than drunk, I think. I've said I'll take him back to college, talk to him about whatever it is, do what I can for him. You'll have to go back alone, I'm afraid."

She did not protest. I think she was already afraid of Atherton, of the darkness that seemed to surround him.

"You will not be long?" she asked, and I could sense the thin patina of fear on her voice.

I shook my head.

"Not above an hour, I promise."

I took them to the front gate, where a fly was already waiting by prior arrangement. Once they were settled and started off, I returned to find Atherton.

He had squeezed himself inside the doorway of the first staircase in the Gibbs Building, where he stood casting his eyes over everything that moved, whether from the chapel to his left or across the lawn in front of him. It was the dead time of day, between evensong and hall. The congregation had gone, and few people were at large in the college grounds. A heavy stillness lay across everything.

Catching sight of me, Atherton came out, and attached himself to my arm as before, making me an anchorage for his fears.

"I can't spend long," I said. "My wife will be waiting for me."

We skirted the lawn and came out on to King's Parade. From there, I would normally have made my way to Sidney Sussex by way of Bene't Street, through the market place, and down through Petty Cury. But Atherton would not hear of such a route, preferring instead to stick to the better lighted streets as far as St John's, turning back there at the top of Sidney Street, and so down to Sidney Sussex.

He was silent for most of our walk, but all the time kept glancing round, as though he saw something in this corner or that. His shambling gait attracted the attention of a few passers-by, but no one known to either of us was among them. I led him thus, like one leading a drunken man home after a party.

Once safely inside his rooms, he locked and bolted the door, and closed the shutters across all his windows. He would not say a word to me until he had done that and assured himself that each of his rooms in turn was empty. Back in the sitting room, he turned the gas-lights up full and sat down at last, face to face with me in a thickly padded leather armchair that smelled of endless tutorial sessions spent wrestling with Greek verbs.

On a small table beside the chair sat a cut-glass decanter and a heavy tumbler. Atherton proceeded to pour himself half a glass of whisky. He held the decanter out to me, but I shook my head and he set it down again.

"Do you think that's entirely wise?" I asked.

By way of reply, he drained the glass in a single mouthful. He looked at me defiantly as he put the glass back on the table.

"She's very pretty, your wife," he said. "You're a lucky man."

"Thank you. I'm sorry I did not introduce you, but—"

"Don't bother explaining. You must find it shaming to have friends such as me."

"Come now, don't be absurd."

"And the boy too. Her child, obviously. A charming boy, and pretty like his mother . . ."

His voice trailed away, and for a brief interval I lost him, as though his mind had momentarily gone in search of something. Memories, perhaps. Likenesses. Other charming boys born of pretty mothers. I realised how little I knew of Atherton.

"Why have you come looking for me?" I asked.

He stirred, coming back from wherever he had been.

"I've already told you," he said. His words came in jerks, as though forced out at intervals by thoughts he was unable to control. "Too many shadows. You don't see them at first, you can't . . . not if you're looking directly at them. Really, they're all one shadow . . . just one shadow multiplied. Does that make sense? Perhaps it doesn't . . . in our world. But we aren't in our . . . cosy little world any longer, are we, Asquith? We're in . . . his world, we're . . . his creatures, he makes us what we are. Eh, Asquith? You've seen him too, haven't you? He's . . . followed you as well."

For all their stumbling incoherence, his words made the deepest possible impact on me. I had seen the shadow he spoke of, after all – and more than just a shadow.

"Calm down, Atherton," I said. "Tell me exactly what you think you've seen."

He seemed to hesitate, as though my demand for exactitude threatened the imprecision with which he was protecting himself.

"A shadow, don't you see?" he began at last. "That's . . . all I thought it was at first. Following me everywhere. I saw it . . . I saw it the first time in the Fellows' Garden. It wasn't . . . apparent at first. Not to the naked eye. There was a little . . . sunlight, you see, some . . . shadows from the trees, nothing out of the ordinary. And then . . . I'm not sure . . . out of the corner of my eye . . . a shadow that . . . should not have been there. Do you understand? I . . . don't know how I knew. I . . . looked away, just briefly, and when I looked back it had gone. I thought it nothing. Just a trick of the light, you see. An autumn shadow, between noon and sunset. But . . . it should not have been there . . ."

"You've been under terrible strain," I said, lamely falling back on the weakest of explanations. "The autumn light plays tricks, exaggerates distances—"

"Don't patronise me, Asquith. Don't do that, please. I know what I saw. Then and afterwards. I . . . saw it the second time in hall, a shadow moving when the candlelight was still. It was as black as soot, a . . . misshapen thing – but I knew it could take on shape if it wanted. The third time was near this building, at the foot of my staircase, next to Burridge's room. It was waiting quietly for me to go upstairs. That was last night. I've kept it out since then, but I know it's waiting. *Evigilavit adversum te ecce venit."*

He paused, then reached forward and grabbed me hard again by the upper arm.

"You must tell me what to do," he cried. "You have to help me keep it out."

I remembered the text he had just quoted, and the lines that preceded it, words blacked out by Edward Atherton: *haec dicit Dominus Deus adflictio una adflictio ecce venit; finis venit venit finis; evigilavit adversum te ecce venit.* 'Thus saith the

Lord God; An evil, an only evil, behold is come. An end is come, the end is come; it watcheth for thee; behold, it is come.'
I shuddered, in spite of my need to preserve what appearances remained to me.

"How long ago is it since you saw him first?" I asked.

"Five days ago, or thereabouts."

"Then you're in no immediate danger. There's nothing I can do for you tonight. This whole business must be tackled at its source. Stay in your rooms. Don't go out for any reason. I'll come back in the morning, and we'll go to Thornham St Stephen together. Lethaby must be made to see reason."

"Can't you stay here?" he pleaded.

I shook my head.

"It's out of the question. I have to think of my family. Don't worry, the night will pass. Nothing will happen. Nothing will come."

He remained unconvinced, and I continued to do my best to reassure him. In the end I succeeded enough to make him agree to see the thing through till the morning. He would, I knew, drink himself into a stupor anyway. Had it not been for the shadow I had seen at Ullswater, I might have put it all down to whisky. Even now, I was not sure Atherton had seen more than alcohol-induced phantasms.

He accompanied me to the door, pathetically trusting now, like a dog reassured by a careless master. My mind, I confess, was set more on the problems of finding a cab and getting home than on Atherton and his shadows. I turned as I left, and saw his pale face wedged in the crack of the doorway, his watery eyes fixed on me, as though to hold me to all my promises. Next moment, the face had gone, and I heard the sound of a key being turned hard in the lock.

The staircase was ill lit. I hurried down it and out into the

151

court beyond, barely pausing to look into the shadows at the foot of the stairs, the spot where Atherton had fancied he saw something lurking.

The night will pass. Nothing will happen. Nothing will come.

God forgive me for those words, for the rashness and arrogance of them. Had I not spoken them, all might have turned out differently.

But I had already half forgotten them by the time I reached the open air. I did not look behind me, but scurried out of Sidney Sussex, past the porters' lodge and into the street. It was dark, there were shadows on the moon, and a cold wind was blowing from across the fens.

Twenty

S imone fell ill that night. I was awakened around two o'clock in the morning, I'm not sure by what. I remember that I had been dreaming vividly, and not, I think, of pleasant things. It took me some moments, therefore, to recover myself and to come fully awake.

When I did so, I noticed that Simone was breathing heavily, and when I moved towards her, she let out a groan.

"What's wrong?" I asked. It was pitch dark, and I could see nothing.

"Hard . . . to breathe . . . Tried . . . to wake you."

I fumbled for a match and lit the candle I always keep by the bedside table. When I brought the light close to her, I could see that Simone was flushed and sweating heavily, her chest rising and falling violently in her efforts to breathe. I rose at once and, waking Ned, sent him at once to Dr Willingham, a local man who attended my sister and her family. His house was not far from ours, and he arrived some twenty minutes later, rather put out to be wakened at such an hour by someone he had not previously met.

He was a bustling man of about forty, stocky, a little overweight, yet elegant in all he did. I thought him daunting at first, for he made it clear the moment he set foot inside the house that he would brook no careless waste of his time. His still, watery eyes betrayed both intelligence and impatience. He was not a man to suffer fools gladly. Nor, I sensed at once, was he a man who would stint in anything could he but save his patient.

His manner changed on seeing Simone, and he set about examining her scrupulously while I relayed questions in French. This took about ten minutes. At the end of this period, Willingham scribbled some notes on a scrap of paper and sent Ned off to his house to fetch various medicines and powders. While we were awaiting Ned's return, the doctor took me aside.

"Professor Asquith, I must confess that I am really at a loss to explain your wife's condition. She has a high fever, her pulse is rapid, and her breathing is abnormally laboured. Has she been under any particular strain recently? Any excitement out of the ordinary?"

I explained that she had been bereaved, and that she and I had only recently married. Willingham shook his head.

"Yes, it's highly possible that the rapid change in circumstances following a period of mourning may have provoked a nervous reaction. I'll give her some morphine to steady her nerves. I find it much safer than pure opium or laudanum. She'll also need something to bring down that fever. Watch her closely for the next few hours. I'll come back later in the morning."

I did not close my eyes all night. Soon after the morphine had been administered, Simone fell into a deep sleep. Nevertheless, I did not allow myself to do the same. For the first time in my life, I had someone to watch over. From time to time, if I looked up, I would see shadows in the corners of the room, and for the first time since I was a child, I prayed. Against the gathering darkness, against death, against the loss of what we love.

Bertrand too remained sleepless, although Dr Willingham's visit had done much to reassure him. The doctor had taken him aside and spoken to him, trying to convince him that all was well, and that his mother would recover soon. I also spoke with him, but I fear I was less convincing, for I shared his fears and dreaded any worsening of Simone's condition.

Throughout all this, Atherton and his troubles were not forgotten. If I closed my eyes for a moment, I could see him skulking in his room alone, in mortal terror of something he had but partly glimpsed. My own fears, however, were more immediate, and I would open my eyes and gaze down at Simone's sleeping form, so still on the bed beside me, and so utterly precious.

She woke again shortly after eleven. The heavy curtains were still drawn, and a fresh candle was burning by the bedside. I had fallen into a light doze, but grew alert the moment I felt her stir beside me. For several moments, she seemed confused and frightened, still partly in a stupor as a result of the morphine. I reached forward to calm her, and, as I did so, she stared directly at me, and I swear that, for some brief moments, what looked out at me from her eyes was not my wife, but someone else entirely. She blinked, and it was Simone again, her eyes filled with fear and incomprehension. I held her to me, and she came into my arms moaning gently and mumbling words I could not make out.

Dr Willingham arrived about half an hour later. By then, Simone was showing signs of recovery, though still much weakened by her fever. The doctor examined her carefully again. When he was done, he reassured her that all was well, but insisted she rest for the remainder of the day, and eat only light dishes for the next week or so. He prescribed a tonic and left a small bottle of pills 'to help her nerves'.

Before leaving, he took me aside to say that, though Simone's recovery seemed complete, he remained puzzled by the whole thing.

"It may be nothing more than a short-lived reaction to the rapid change of circumstances you told me of, in which case I see no grounds for apprehension. She seems perfectly well now, and her constitution seems extremely robust. Nevertheless, I make it a rule never to be complacent in such matters. Your wife must be watched with care for the next few weeks. Report to me any changes, however slight. We may be able to prevent a second attack before it gets under way. I'll make calls at your house every other day for the first week or so. And be sure she takes her tonic religiously."

Soon after his departure, Agnes arrived on our doorstep, having heard only minutes earlier from Willingham's wife the nature of his mid-morning errand. She scolded me for not having called her in the night, and went up straight away to sit with Simone.

I took advantage of her being there to accompany Bertrand to school, for I thought it best he stick as near as possible to his original plan. We had acquired a pair of Stanley safety bicycles, and I had taught Bertrand to ride. It was raining lightly that morning, but we made good time and were at the choir school by lunchtime. I explained the reason for Bertrand's absence and left him in the capable hands of M. Aristide, whose charge he was to remain for the first month or so. It was arranged that I should collect him after choir practice that evening.

As I rode away from the school, my thoughts turned to Atherton and my promise. To be honest, I was sorely tempted to ignore him and return to Simone, whose condition continued to cause me anxiety, despite Willingham and his reassurances. But, as always, Atherton exercised a hold over me. Perhaps it was pity, perhaps a sense of duty. And perhaps it was no more than the revulsion I felt at my own distaste for the man. His fear was, after all, no more than an exaggeration and perversion of my own. I had Simone to comfort me, he had no one.

I cycled the short distance to Sidney Sussex and, leaving my bicycle with the porter (who insisted that no such 'contrivance' might pass within the inner sancta of the college), made my way to the building in which Atherton had rooms. The paths were packed with black-gowned college men who had just come from lunch in hall and were now heading off for afternoon lectures, to dreary hours with tutors, or to the silent contemplation of the whisky bottle in their own chambers. There was a solemn, almost monastic feeling about the place, or perhaps it was just an alteration in my own perception of things, occasioned by my marriage and my new-found domesticity.

Atherton's staircase, though lit through a series of long windows on each landing, had a dim, oppressive character, an air of neglect that made it seem cauled in a permanent shadow. There are stairs like that in every college, ill-positioned and destined to become the abode of the most reclusive dons and the least popular undergraduates. Dark, faintly smelling of mould and long, sinking illnesses, they draw to themselves whatever misery may be found in the closed, stagnant world around them.

Atherton's stair had its own quality besides, a quality of menace, of foreboding. I disliked being there intensely, and as I climbed the stairs I found myself again glancing uneasily into their dark corners.

I knocked on Atherton's door, but there was no response. Again and again I knocked, but once the sound died away, a weary silence returned. The shadows and the curious angles of the staircase swallowed up even the echoes and left me bleak and frightened outside the unopened door.

Retracing my steps to the porter's lodge, I enquired if Dr Atherton was expected back that afternoon. The porter, a rubicund man whose careworn manner flatly contradicted his cherubic features, gave me a puzzled look.

"Dr Atherton? Well, sir, he usually keeps to his rooms on Thursdays. Has done for years. No outside classes, tutorials every other hour. Myself, I've been on duty here since eight o'clock this morning, and I'm sure I ain't seen him go past."

He crossed to the other side of his little enclave and glanced at the pigeon-holes lined up against the wall. When he came back, the puzzlement on his face had deepened into something like concern.

"Hasn't been for his letters neither, sir. I reckon he's still in his rooms. I'd come with you, sir, but my orders are strict, and I daren't leave my place here. You'll find Dr Atherton's skip on Y staircase, first door on the left. He has the key."

As I turned apprehensively to go, the porter called after me.

"I hope nothing's wrong," he said. "God forbid he's been took ill."

I hardly answered, so preoccupied was I and so loud was the beating of my craven heart in my own breast.

Rawles, the skip, was in his store-room as predicted, sorting laundry. I explained what had happened. He straightened up, a slender man with callused hands and a sad face.

"Not answering, you say?"

I shook my head.

"Not at all like him. Sharp ears, has Dr Atherton."

He opened a large cupboard and took down a large ring of keys from a rusty hook.

"Sharp ears," he repeated. "Very prompt. Some think him a dull man, a quiet man, but I find him sharp as nails."

I accompanied him to Atherton's stair, regaled at first by observations on various aspects of my friend's character. As we drew closer, however, my silence and my mood of disquiet must have insinuated themselves into Rawles's consciousness, and we climbed the stairs without a word between us.

Rawles knocked as I had done, but had no more answer than myself. He called a few times, at first in a quiet, respectful voice, then more loudly. I feared the worst by now, and told Rawles he must open the door.

"I'm not sure as it's my place without permission, sir. You're not a Fellow of this college, and I've no authority to go opening doors without by or leave."

"He may be ill. I saw him last night, and he looked poorly then. If you don't open the door, I'll break it down myself."

This threat had the desired effect. Rawles opened the door and let it swing back into the room. It was pitch dark inside, for the shutters and curtains were still drawn. A strange smell struck my nostrils at once, as though the room had been shut up for a very long time. I recognised it straight away as the same smell that I had met when entering Atherton's mother's room all those weeks earlier. Rawles noticed it too. I saw him hesitate at the threshold and clap one hand to his mouth.

"Rawles," I said, "find a light as quick as you can." Nothing could have induced me to go any further into that room without first having at least a candle with which to light my way.

Rawles took a box of matches from his waistcoat pocket and slipped round the door. He knew exactly where to find the nearest gas mantle, and in moments he had it lit. A dull yellow light quickened and settled.

I do not know quite what I had expected to find. Atherton

crouching on the floor, perhaps, a quivering wreck. Or Atherton stretched out on his bed like his brother or mother before him, terror written across his face in bold letters. But no such sight greeted me, neither in the living room nor the bedroom, nor in the small study to one side. The rooms were quite empty. Of Atherton there was not the slightest trace.

Rawles opened the windows to let in both light and air. Able to see properly, he and I made a quick examination of the rooms.

"I think he's gone out after all, sir. We'd better lock up and wait till he comes back."

"No," I said. "Something's wrong. That dreadful smell. It wasn't here last night."

Had it not been for the odour pervading everything and only slowly dispersing as fresh air entered the rooms, I think Rawles would have hustled me through the door that moment. Moreover, it was immediately obvious that Atherton had left the place in a terrible mess, quite unlike its normal state. Books and papers were piled everywhere, strewn across the floor and heaped on tables and chairs. I picked up a sheet of paper. Across it someone – Atherton I presumed – had scribbled strings of letters and numbers. And so on every sheet I lifted. The same letters, marked with different figures, or in different combinations. By the third or fourth sheet I realised that he had been trying to decode the random letters carved on William de Lindesey's tomb.

It was Rawles who found the next puzzling item: Atherton's door key, set on the little table by the door where he always kept it. But the door had been locked from the inside when we arrived.

"Did he keep another set?" I asked.

Rawles shook his head.

"I don't think so, sir. If he was ever to lose a key when out, he knew he could have another from me or the porter."

"He can't have left by the window."

"No, sir, you're right. All shuttered, sir, all closed tight."

"Maybe he had another key cut. To give to a friend, perhaps. Some men let graduates use their rooms in their absence. Dr Atherton has a fine collection of books."

"I'm sure you're right, sir."

I nodded, but I knew the truth was quite different. Matthew Atherton had not left his rooms after I took my leave of him. I picked up more of the scattered sheets. On some, the paper was torn where Atherton's pen had gouged holes.

"Leave those, sir," said Rawles. "I'll tidy them later on."

"If you don't mind, I'd like to keep them for a day or two. Dr Atherton won't mind. They're for a lecture I'm working on. He was helping me with it last night – I called back for my papers this morning: I need to work on them today. Just say Professor Asquith took them."

Though it was evident he had misgivings, Rawles acquiesced. It was only a matter of a few sheets of paper, after all.

Though the smell had largely disappeared, I still felt acute uneasiness in that place. Several sheets had been left in the bedroom. I went in to fetch them and, as I did so, noticed that the bedclothes had been pulled back and were tangled together, as though someone had spent a restless night then leapt from bed suddenly.

Going closer to pick up a sheet of paper that had fallen by the side of the bed, I noticed something that had earlier escaped my attention. A long brown stain lay on the undersheet, as long as a man, and about as broad. One part of the stain revealed the unmistakable imprint of a human hand. And I noticed that some of the same stain covered the pillow.

Rawles, who had followed me into the room, noticed it too.

"Whatever's that?" he asked. "Those sheets were fresh only two days ago."

I went no closer. The stain seemed to me an unclean thing; I could not bear to touch it or look at it any longer. Gathering the loose papers in my hand, I apologised to Rawles for having inconvenienced him, and hurried out, not pausing to close the door behind me.

Twenty-One

S imone woke me again that night. Exhausted by my vigil of the morning before, and the anxiety provoked by my visit to Atherton's rooms, I had fallen into a deep sleep marred by disturbing dreams. I woke to find Simone clutching my arm. She had shaken me to consciousness, terrified by a dream of her own.

I lit the oil-lamp and turned to reassure her. She was pale and trembling, like someone who has received a sudden shock.

"What's wrong?" I asked, fearing she was about to have a relapse, that her fever had returned, perhaps more virulent than before.

She could not answer me at once. I reached out and touched her; her skin was cold. I waited patiently.

"I was there again," she said at last.

"There?"

"In that place, the place you took me to. I've been there every night."

My heart felt cold, as though something in it had been extinguished. Simone's pallor frightened and unmanned me more than her burning fever had ever done.

"What place? Where did I take you?"

"To the abbey, the ruined abbey. Thornham."

The cold leapt from my heart to the rest of my body.

"You dream of Thornham Abbey?"

"Yes, often. I did not tell you, it did not seem important. But tonight was . . . different. Tonight was horrible."

"I don't understand. What did you see in this dream?"

She looked round suddenly, as though some sound had distracted her, then shivered and returned her gaze to me.

"Until tonight," she said, faltering, her eyes fixed on me as if to anchor herself to me, "nothing changed, nothing altered. The abbey was just as I remember it from the day of our picnic. In my dream, I would find myself standing there, in the nave of the church. Ruined walls, empty windows, moss-covered stones – just as it is, just as I remember. And all round, the whole countryside, bleak, empty. No one anywhere, not even a bird in flight. Just empty fields, and trees without leaves, and bare hedges, and a wind blowing cold across it all, the way it does sometimes at home in winter."

"So it is winter in your dream?"

"Always winter. Always cold. Always a black wind."

"Does anything happen?"

She shook her head.

"Not until tonight. I stand in the nave, shivering, watching the sun climb down the sky. It comes out from behind grey clouds, very red, red and yellow together. I can see it through a broken window. It is the only thing that moves."

"And tonight?"

"Tonight I am in the abbey, but it is completely changed. Not a ruin any longer. Every stone in its place again. But I know it is the same place because of the window. I look up and see the sun behind the window, high up in the nave, and there is glass that catches the last light and breaks it up. I go on watching until the light fades and it is dark, completely dark, and when I look away from the window the church is in darkness. Someone has lit candles in the chancel. I think I am alone at first, but slowly I become aware that there is someone else. I feel terribly afraid. I don't know why. Perhaps it is the darkness. Perhaps it is the lights flickering in the chancel."

I stroked her hair. It had fallen across her face like a veil. I pushed it back gently. She smiled and touched my hand. Her fingers were cold, and she still trembled.

"I walk towards the chancel. It is a dream, remember, and I can do nothing, I must go where the dream takes me. All the time, I want to run, but I cannot. It is quiet, there are no sounds; I cannot even hear my own breath, my own heartbeat. When I reach the chancel, it is like ice, colder even than the nave. It's dark all round me, but there are candles in the choir stalls, tall candles here and there. And shadows, shadows like long, restless animals."

She paused. On the wall behind her, her own shadow moved imperceptibly, long and thin and silent. It seemed a very old thing, far older than Simone or myself.

"He is there. At first he is all I see, standing in front of the altar. He is watching me approach."

"He?"

"*M. l'Abbé.* I don't know his name. He has no name. I cannot see his face, it's hidden inside his hood. But I know he is watching me."

"How do you know he is the abbot?"

"I'm not sure. He stands where the abbot should stand. He's tall, he carries himself proudly, there's something about him, a sort of grandeur. But not holiness, that I do not sense. Just pride, even arrogance. I can feel it washing over me. And something else, something I don't like, much worse than the arrogance."

165

She closed her eyes, and a shudder went through her, quick and febrile.

"He stands there so very still," she went on, "and I know his eyes are watching me, but I cannot see them. Then I hear voices. There are monks in the choir, chanting in plainsong, '*Kyrie, fons bonitatis*', soft voices, very solemn, and at first I think, I must be mistaken, nothing bad could happen here, these are men of God, and their abbot must be a man of God. But there is something wrong with the voices, something I do not like.

"I turn and look, and I see hooded men in the choir, their faces in shadow. Just monks, I think, but still something is wrong. And then I understand. This is a dream, remember: no one has told me, but I know what is wrong. The monks are not alive, none of them is alive. I am in a church of dead men."

She stopped, and I drew her to me.

"It's all right," I said. "Don't go on."

"No, I must finish. I stand like that, watching them, for a long time. Or perhaps it is only seconds, I cannot tell. I remember the abbot, and I turn again, but he is no longer there. At that moment, the singing stops. When I look, the choir is empty, as if no one had been there. But the candles are still burning. I am all alone in the darkness. But I know . . ."

I felt her shiver against me, her body suddenly hard and violent.

"I know I shall not be alone for long. Someone is coming. Someone I do not want to see. And then I wake and I am here."

The shivering passed, and she was still. On the wall behind her, her shadow grew still as well.

Twenty-Two

S imone returned to sleep after a short time and did not wake again until morning. I remained with her, but did not sleep. My mind kept wandering into places I had no wish to know. William de Lindesey was reaching out for me and for those I loved. I had to stop him, but I did not know how.

Shortly after breakfast, I took Bertrand to school, then set out for Sidney Sussex again. Matthew Atherton had not returned to his rooms. He had missed a lecture he was due to deliver that morning, and there was general concern in college that something untoward had taken place.

I spent the rest of the day in my rooms at college, taking care of duties I had neglected for some weeks. But my mind was elsewhere, and as soon as I returned to Trumpington that evening, I started work on decoding the inscription around William de Lindesey's tomb.

Atherton had clearly spent hours puzzling over it. Each of the dozens of sheets I had retrieved from his rooms was covered in scribbles, diagrams, and mathematical computations, in which he had attempted to reduce the inscription to some sort of code or cipher. He had written the letters down in columns, horizontally, vertically, and even diagonally, he had written them in reverse order, then in sequences like one, three, five or two, four, six. Nothing seemed to work in any of the three

167

languages that would have been familiar to Abbot William: Latin, medieval French and English.

I went over his jottings carefully, in the hope he had missed something, but after hours of this I was no further forward. Nothing fitted, absolutely nothing. None of the combinations produced by my juggling of letters made even seeming sense in any conceivable language. Yet I could not believe that anyone had gone to such pains merely to inscribe random letters on a tomb.

I worked until dinner time, and again after that until well past midnight. I was the last to retire. The house was silent, and still unfamiliar to me. It had been built towards the end of the last century, and it had been altered very little since then. Gas had been installed a few years earlier, but only on the ground floor.

As I went upstairs, I cradled a candle as usual. My thoughts were crammed with strings of letters and glimmerings of half-finished words and phrases, and I scarcely noticed my surroundings. It was cold in the passageway. I had an odd sensation that the house was empty, that, while I had been working on my inscription, everyone else had gone, leaving me alone. It was an irrational thought, but it gripped me with unexpected force. I began to climb the stairs, wondering if I should find Simone waiting for me, or whether I would enter the bedroom to find it empty.

These fears began to crowd in on me, harder and harder until I could barely breathe. I told myself it was the purest nonsense, that the house was inhabited as it always was. But a sense of emptiness surrounded me, so great I had almost to struggle physically in order to mount the stairs.

I reached the top at last. The long dark passage leading to our bedroom stretched away from me, scarcely visible in the very little light my candle shed. Outside, a high wind had risen, and as I set foot on the landing, I could hear it more distinctly than before, howling past a skylight higher up. The mournful sounds it made in its passing accentuated my sense that all about me was bleak and empty. It was as if all winter and all winter's sadness lay just outside the window, as if the house had been ripped from its foundations and set down among snow and ice in a deserted wilderness.

As I stepped into the passage, I heard, quite distinctly, another sound. It came from somewhere dead ahead of me, and I did not for a moment think it imagination or an echo of the wind above. Someone was standing in the darkness in front of me. The sound I had heard was a low cough.

"Who's there?" I asked, frightened. No one replied.

"Mrs Lumley? . . . Mary? . . . Simone?"

I had no answer. A wind-torn silence held the house imprisoned.

I took a deep breath and stepped forward, holding the candle in front of me. No one. I went on to the end of the passage. It was empty. No door had been opened, there was nowhere else to go.

I opened the door of our bedroom. The gas-light was still lit. Simone was sitting up in bed, waiting for me. She smiled, and all my fears dropped from me. The wind was still roaring outside, but I knew the bed would be warm, a haven for the night at least.

In the morning, two letters arrived in a single envelope from René, one for Simone and one for myself. Simone's contained news of all that happened in St Barthélemy since her departure – which, to be honest, was not very much at all. Mine, on the other hand, began with about a page of rather effusive reflections on his joy at my marriage to his beloved daughter, before moving on to the scholarly matters that had formed the substance of our regular correspondence over the years.

On the last page, almost as an afterthought, he mentioned something of more immediate interest.

"I have not forgotten our delightful visit to the ruins of Thornham Abbey. You will remember that I already knew of Thornham as a daughter establishment of Fleury. Since my return, I have been reading all I can find about the relationship between the two foundations. There are some published records from Fleury itself, and I have had access to papers at the abbey of Ripoll near here, which was much influenced by Fleury in former times. When I have amassed enough of these, I shall send you copies of the most interesting.

"You will, however, be entertained by the following extract from a chronicle for the year 1349.

In the winter of this year there appeared at Fleury a certain Guillaume de Lindesey, who was Abbot of Thornham in England. He was accompanied by an English knight and his lady, whose names are not recorded. This Guillaume, it seems, had spent his noviciate here, and had returned to pray at the shrine of St Benedict. This followed the deaths of the greater part of his brethren in an outbreak of the plague, may God defend all Christian souls from its ravages.

Abbot Guillaume was thought at first to be a pious man, for his knowledge of the scriptures was unsurpassed, and he spent much of every day immersed in reading of the sacred text. But he had not been at Fleury above a month when a rumour began to circulate, namely that he and his companions had brought with them from England a demon of the plague.

For several of the brothers fell ill at that time with fever, and within two months six of them had suffered terrible deaths This was not the true plague, for none showed the signs of it. Neither the abbot nor the knight nor his lady at any time showed themselves infected, yet it was certain they had brought this illness with them, and that it was Satanic in origin.

That it was a demon or a cacodemon that they brought with them has been attested to by several of the brethren, some of them now living, among them Brother Gildas, Brother Hervey, who was then apothecary, Brother Junien, and our Father Abbot himself, Jacques du Mené-Bré. All these said they had at one time or another seen within the abbey a thing moving that was not a man, yet had the appearance of a man's shadow, being very black and low against the ground, quick in movement, though not quite as a man should move.

Brother Junien has told me that he saw its face on one occasion, coming upon it by candlelight close by the cloister, and that he did not sleep afterwards for upwards of a year. And Brother Hervey says he was watching through the infirmary window one moonlit night and saw a long black creature creeping across the inner court. He said nothing of it at the time, thinking it an illusion, a trick of light. But later, when others began to speak of an apparition, he added his voice to theirs.

It was also rumoured that the English lady slept with her husband on one night and with Abbot Guillaume the next, though God knows if this is the truth or idle gossip. However that may be, our Father Abbot required the three to leave Fleury. It is said that, as they departed, Guillaume turned and recited a malediction against our abbey and its

171

people. May God and His Son turn his curses upon his own head, now and for all eternity. *Si Maldis soient ils quil soient ades en pestillence et en mechies de cuer et de corps. amen. Sy maldis soient ils que dieu envoye sur lour biens et sur leur terres feu et flemme en lieu de pluye. et de rouzee. amen. Maldis excommenies entredis anathematysies soient ils. amen. Sy maldis soient ils comme fuit dathan abyron quils pour leurs meffais furent transglutis de la terre tous vis. amen.*

René ended his letter with some amusing remarks about the malediction with which the chronicler had ended his account. I could not laugh at it. I knew how seriously it had been meant; and how ineffective it had been. William and, no doubt, his companions had returned to England and to Thornham, where he had somehow contrived to stay as abbot until his death some nine years later. What had been the fate of Hugh de Warenne and his accommodating lady was a matter for conjecture, but I suspected that they must have insinuated themselves somehow as patrons of Thornham Abbey or of its dower church at Thornham St Stephen. A little further digging in the archives would doubtless reveal the truth, or as much of it as might have been recorded.

It was that same afternoon that Mrs Lumley came to me while I was working in my study, an expression of the most lively consternation on her usually placid face.

"Whatever's the matter, Mrs Lumley?" I asked, putting down my pen and preparing myself for my first domestic tragedy. I knew she was reluctant to bring household matters to Simone on account of the language barrier between them.

"It's Mary, sir."

"Yes, what about her?"

"She's packing her things, sir, and says she means to leave the house at once."

"Whatever can have happened?"

Mrs Lumley spread her very ample hands in a gesture worthy of a Mediterranean matron.

"That I can't say for the life of me, sir, except that she swears she will not spend another night under this roof."

It was then that I remembered with sickening vividness my own experience of the night before. Had Mary too heard or seen something?

"Ask her to come here at once, Mrs Lumley. I'd like to have a word with her."

"She says she won't speak to anyone, sir. She doesn't care about a reference, all she wants is to leave. I can't make rhyme nor reason of it, that I can't, sir."

"All the same, ask her to come down. Tell her I'm not angry and I won't stop her leaving. But I would like to speak with her, if she doesn't mind."

Mrs Lumley cast me a look at once quizzical and disapproving, as though she suspected me personally of being the cause of the maid's precipitate departure. Clamping her mouth firmly shut on whatever remark she was about to make, she turned on her heels and hurried upstairs. A few minutes later, an abashed and nervous Mary appeared in the study. She appeared ashamed, frightened, and anxious, yet the look in her eyes was unmistakably one of resolution.

"Mrs Lumley tells me you wish to leave, Mary. Is that true?"

"Yes, sir. I'm sorry, sir, but it is true."

Her voice shook, but she forced the words out with a determination I could only admire.

"This is very sudden. Is there a reason? Has something happened?"

She pressed her lips tightly together and shook her head, then, unable to hold out any longer, burst into tears.

"It's all right, Mary, no one's going to get angry with you. If you're really set on leaving us, you may have your wages and a letter of recommendation. You've been a good girl, and we shall be sad to see you go. But I would like to know if anything has happened to bring you to such a sudden decision. Is it your family? Can we do anything to help?"

She calmed down slowly, affected, I think, by words of kindness she had little expected. Whipping out a handkerchief from the end of one sleeve, she wiped her eyes.

"It's no good, sir, I've tried, truly I have, but it's more than I can bear. If I don't leave today, I know I'll go mad. I can't spend another night in that room, God knows I can't."

"I don't understand, Mary. What's more than you can bear? Is something the matter with your room?"

She nodded.

"That's just it, sir. It's not my room, for it's a very nice room, and sorry I am to have to give it up, but it's right next to the main attic, sir."

The main attic was a large empty space beneath the roof, where we kept trunks and papers for which there was no room in my study. It was a draughty, echoing place, long unused, and filled with dust and cobwebs.

"Don't you like that?"

"I didn't mind it at first, sir. It's only an attic, after all. But then . . ."

"Yes?"

"Then the noises started, sir."

My heart ground to a halt, then started to beat again, slowly and unpleasantly.

"Noises?" I repeated.

"In the attic, sir. Like people talking, but low, so you can't make nothing out. They've been there for nights, sir. I put up with them at first, thinking they might be what you call echoes, from underneath, perhaps. Sounds travel in big houses like this. There are pipes and that. But last night . . ."

Her voice trailed away, and when she looked at me I could see genuine fear in her eyes.

"Last night? What happened then?"

A very great reluctance came over her then, a manifest aversion to speak of whatever it was she had seen or heard.

"It's all right, Mary. This is in confidence. I won't tell a soul."

"It's not that, sir. I just don't like to talk about it. You'll think I'm making up stories."

I shook my head.

"No, Mary, I won't think anything of the sort. I believe you're telling the truth."

My mood somehow reached out to her, and I think she sensed I knew more than she had at first imagined.

"Well, sir, what it was last night, sir . . . I heard singing. In the attic, like before, only singing as it were, not talking."

"But surely . . . Was that so frightening?"

"Yes, sir, it was. Worse than anything, sir. It wasn't quite singing. Not songs as such, sir."

"I don't understand what you mean."

She hesitated, trying to find the right words for what she wanted to say.

"What it was like, sir, was a sort of hymn, only not the sort they sing in church. I have an aunt Beatrice, very proper and a bit stuck up, but awful religious. Aunt Bea doesn't hold with ordinary churches, she'd rather travel miles for what she calls High Church. Incense and suchlike. She's as near a Catholic as makes no difference, though she calls herself Church of England like the rest of us. Not that there's anything wrong with Catholics, sir – your good lady being one, as I know."

"Go on, Mary. What has your aunt Beatrice to do with all this?"

"Only this, sir. When I was small, she'd take me now and then to Walsingham, to the Shrine of Our Lady. There are two shrines, as you may know, sir, a Catholic shrine and one of our own. Mostly we'd go to our own shrine, but sometimes Aunt Beatrice would go to the Catholics and sit for a while. That's where I heard that singing, sir. Singing that's not really singing, just sort of up and down, and terrible solemn."

"Plainsong."

She nodded.

"That's right, sir. That's what my aunt called it. It was sung by monks. And that's what I heard last night, sir. Someone all alone, singing to himself. It went on all night till I thought I'd go mad of it."

Twenty-Three

I could not prevail on Mary to stay, nor did I feel it in my heart to try very hard. Given the chance, I should have packed all our bags and taken us from the house at once, were it not for the fact that I knew he would follow us wherever we went, that flight from him was impossible. Our only hope lay in his defeat, in his final, unequivocal destruction. And I still did not know how I was to accomplish that.

I explained to Simone that Mary had left on account of difficulties at home, where her services were required to nurse a sick relative. Mrs Lumley agreed to find another girl to take her place on Monday. In the meantime, Simone was perfectly happy to take care of Mary's chores herself, or with Mrs Lumley's assistance.

After lunch, she took Bertrand for a walk along the river, down to Byron's Pool and across to Grantchester. I cried off, saying I had urgent work to do. Mrs Lumley would be busy in the kitchen, and young Ned had work in the garden, sweeping up mounds of fallen leaves. While they were both occupied, I intended to pay a visit to the attic, though what precisely I hoped or feared to find there I did not know.

It was still light when I closed the door of my study gently and headed upstairs. All the same, my memories of climbing those same stairs in the darkness not many hours before clung to me tenaciously and came close to driving me back down again. Only the thought of Simone and my fears for her safety lent me the resolution to proceed. But for Mrs Lumley, far out of hearing in her hot domain at the back of the house, the place was entirely empty now, just as I had imagined it the night before.

A single enclosed flight of uncarpeted stairs led up to the attic floor. I confess I stood at the bottom for a long time before mustering up the courage to go a step further. All the time I remained there I listened intently for the sound of chanting that Mary had described, but I could hear nothing but the occasional noises any old house makes as its timbers settle in the cooling of the day.

In the end, I could stand the waiting no longer. At the top of the stairs I lit the oil lamp I had brought with me and opened the door.

Soft light fell through a sloping window in the roof. My own light comforted me for all that. A short passage led to the main attic door. On either side were the rooms belonging to Mrs Lumley and, until today, Mary. The cook's was the larger, extending into the eaves and connecting only narrowly with the attic proper. Mary's, on my right, had all of its back wall and most of one side wall against the empty space beyond.

Mary had said that the sounds came from the long attic room that took up the remainder of the space beneath the roof. I went there now, opening the door quickly, knowing I would lose courage should I hesitate.

The skylights here were dirty, letting in very little illumination. I was more grateful than ever for the lamp I carried. The attic was a cobwebbed, dusty place, full of little muffled echoes. As I entered, I recited a prayer for protection from spiritual danger. In recent days, my unbelief had suffered heavy blows.

It was very cold. Though the roof was well tiled, draughts passed through that empty space with little impediment. I raised my lamp and shone it all about me. Trunks, wooden boxes, tea-chests, some items of furniture we had disliked and relegated to this oubliette – all tumbled together in a state of confusion, waiting for a day when someone would find time to tidy them. I held my breath lest something move, but nothing did. I expected at any moment to hear a voice, but the deep silence continued uninterrupted.

I walked round slowly, searching for some indication of what might have caused the sounds that had frightened young Mary. It was not impossible, I tried to persuade myself, that what she had heard had been nothing more than the cooing of pigeons, or the cries of some other animal, transformed to human speech by a vivid imagination. But of living creatures I saw no sign, save for some mouse droppings and the dried excrement of birds. This latter I took as evidence that pigeons might well have been here recently.

Just as I was about to leave, I noticed something on the ground near the door. I took it at first for a dead mouse or something of the kind, and made to pass it at a little distance. Looking more closely, however, I saw it was nothing more than a scrap of black rag, very like the piece Simone had picked up outside our chalet in the Lakes. I did not bend to touch it.

As I shut the door of the main attic, it occurred to me that it might be worth my while looking into the room in which Mary had been sleeping. I thought perhaps I might find some clue as to the source of the sounds she had heard. Even then I was still desperate to find a rational explanation.

I opened the door of the little bedchamber and went in. My first impression was that the room was empty. Mary's paltry possessions had been taken away, leaving the walls bare and the dressing-table unfurnished. As I stepped further into the room, however, letting the door close behind me, I caught sight of something on the bed. Something white. Something unmoving.

And then it moved. Tendrils curled about my heart, choking it. I very nearly screamed. But the white thing on the bed lifted itself and turned, and as it did so I realised it was Mary. She must not have left after all, but had returned to her room to sleep. She was dressed in nothing but a shift, and it crossed my mind that she must have been cold up here.

"Professor Asquith." She was the first to speak, for I was still frozen with fear. "What are you doing here?"

"I . . . I was going to ask you the same thing. Have you changed your mind after all?"

"I felt tired, sir. I came up for a sleep."

She lifted herself further, arching her back as she slid to the side of the bed. Her hair was untied, and it fell down her back and across her slim shoulders. It was long and luxuriant, darker than I remembered it. But I had not seen it untied before. I became uncomfortably conscious of her state of undress, of the impropriety of my being there.

"I'm sorry, Mary, I should not have disturbed you. Do you mean to stay on?"

"Of course I do, sir. You don't want me to leave, do you sir?"

"I've already said so. We'll bring your things up again later. But I shouldn't be here in your room. I only came to see it was tidy."

"There's no need to apologise, sir." She moved her head to

one side, and her hair fell back, exposing her neck and the edges of her shoulders. I felt myself blush.

"I think it's better I should go. I'll be downstairs when you're ready."

Before I could turn to go, Mary stood.

"There's no need to go, sir. I'd like you to stay. Really I would, sir."

Saying this, she reached down and lifted her shift and pulled it over her head in a single, rapid movement. She held it for a moment in one hand, then dropped it and tilted her head so that her hair fell back with it and left her quite naked.

I am not a sensual man. Until I married Simone, I had not slept with a woman nor seen one naked in the flesh. I was not unaware of this woman's good looks or that one's figure, but I never accorded such things the importance I knew some other men did, and I had never let my life be disrupted by them. My lack of that pleasure did not trouble me greatly in my youth, and in later life I was well accustomed to it.

In the short time that I had been married, however, I had come to understand how a man could be so drawn to a woman as to lose his mind in pursuit of her. It had been an emotional and physical awakening, the first time in my life I had discovered the body to be fiercer than the mind, and more fulfilling. In only weeks, my senses had undergone a transformation fully as great as that my heart had known months earlier, when I first acknowledged that I loved Simone.

I will now confess that it was this keen awareness of what was beautiful in a woman that prevented me from acting as I should have done, and dashing from the room. Mary's body was exquisite, just as I might, in an unguarded moment, have imagined it for myself. She possessed the nubile perfection common to so many girls of fifteen or sixteen, when the grossness that may later mar their form is still some years away. Her little breasts and narrow, fluted hips seemed to me at that moment objects of the most inexpressible desire. I could not help but look at her, and she could not fail to see the spark of interest in my eyes.

It was only with the most extreme exertion of my will that I was able to prevent the whole incident descending to yet deeper levels of infamy.

"Mary, this is outrageous! Put your shift back on at once! You don't know what you're doing."

She laughed and took a step closer to me.

"Oh, that I do, sir. I knows exactly what I'm doing."

"What if someone found us like this? What would they think? Mrs Lumley could come in. Or my wife."

She laughed again, and as she did so ran her hands across her breasts and down the front of her body. I could not take my eyes away, and I knew that if I stayed a moment longer I was lost.

"Why, Mrs Asquith won't be back for ages yet, sir. No one'll find us here. No one need know. Just take your clothes off, sir, and we'll have a little fun. I've always had a liking for you, sir, and I know you've had a fancy for me."

She was only a foot or two away, close enough to reach out and touch, close enough to smell.

Only then, in that moment before I took full leave of my senses, before my hand reached out to touch her and pull her to me, did I smell what must have been there all along. Not a young woman's perfume, nor the smell of her unperfumed body, but that rank odour of decay I had encountered twice before, most recently in Atherton's rooms.

I took a step back, and another, until my shoulders were pressing against the door.

"You're not Mary," I said.

She seemed to freeze. The smile that had been on her lips faded and was replaced by something else, something much less enticing. She started to take a step towards me, raising her arms as though to draw me to her, but I spoke the first words of the prayer I had used earlier: *"Domine Deus meus in te speravi salvum me fac ex omnibus persequentibus me et libera me . . ."*

I do not know exactly what happened next. The thing that had taken Mary's form let out a most terrible cry, a cry that was neither human nor animal. I watched it back away, but even as it did so, all resemblance to poor Mary was vanishing from it. The white skin it had impersonated grew suddenly black, and the whole form seemed to shrink.

I must have fainted then. All I remember is coming to in Mary's empty room, my nostrils still stinging with that fearful odour, now stronger than ever. I picked myself up, turned, and stumbled from the room.

As I reached the next floor, I heard a voice calling my name. Mrs Lumley was crying loudly, and I could tell at once that something was wrong. I hurried down the stairs and found her running along the hallway, calling for me in a state of great distress.

"Mrs Lumley? Whatever's going on? What's the matter?"

She looked up and caught sight of me.

"Oh, sir, do come quickly. It's something dreadful."

I thought at once that something must have happened to Simone, that she was dead or injured. And to think that, moments earlier . . .

"It's Master Bertrand, sir. He's been near as drowned. They

brought him home a few minutes ago. His poor mother's in a dreadful state."

Bertrand had already been brought indoors and laid on a sofa in the morning room. Ned had run to fetch Dr Willingham, while Simone remained with the boy. She and Mrs Lumley had already stripped him of his clothes, which lay in a soaking pile near him on the floor. He was wrapped in warm blankets, and Simone was trying to make him drink brandy from a tumbler. Her hand was shaking so much she could barely hold the glass steady against his lips. He was pale and shaking, but at least he was alive.

"Good God, Simone. What happened?"

I crouched beside her, taking her in my arms and holding her to me tightly. She twisted round, pressing herself against me and bursting into tears. For minutes she was convulsed by them, great gulping sobs that wracked her body and almost prevented her from breathing. I soothed and stroked her, calming her bit by bit until she was able to speak.

"Bertrand . . . fell into the water. It was . . . very deep. He . . . he can't swim. His head went under, he . . . he started to drown . . ."

She looked at me, and in her eyes I saw an expression so despairing I could not bear to see it. I pressed her against me again and let her go on weeping. She recovered after a bit and went on.

"I tried to reach him, but I can't swim either, and the only stick I could find was too short. Then two men came running. One . . . jumped in, the other held me back. The one who went into the water . . . brought Bertrand out. I . . . thought he was dead. He was . . . so still . . . so . . . quiet."

"How long was he in the water?"

She shook her head.

"I don't know . . . It seemed to last for ever."

"And the men?"

"They carried him back here. I think . . . they're in the kitchen. The one who rescued Bertrand was wet. Mrs Lumley said she'd find him some warm clothes."

"Let me deal with that."

Simone returned to Bertrand, who was conscious, but badly frightened and unable to talk. She stroked his forehead and whispered gently to him. I thought of the thing I had seen upstairs. I thought of the desire it had aroused in me.

At that moment Dr Willingham arrived. He had been at the house only that morning, to check on Simone, and his first thought on being summoned back was that she had suffered a relapse.

As he started to examine Bertrand, I took Simone from the room. Her skirts were wet where she had waded some way into the water in her vain attempt to rescue her son. I told Mrs Lumley to help her upstairs, while I went to the kitchen to speak with Bertrand's rescuers.

They turned out to be students, two rowing men from Clare who had been walking along the towpath to examine the lie of the river in preparation for a coming race. I thanked them effusively and saw to it that the lad who'd jumped in was brought warm towels and clothes from my wardrobe. Mrs Lumley, calmer now that the doctor was there, busied herself making hot toddies, beef tea, and buttered toast.

The students, whose names were Radcliffe and Elliot, made light of the affair, other than to enquire solicitously after Bertrand.

"His mother and I owe you his life," I said. "I can never repay you. If you hadn't been there at that moment, he would certainly have drowned."

"It was a stroke of good luck," said Elliot, who had held Simone back from plunging further in and, in all probability, compounding the tragedy. "We were debating whether to turn back or head on for Grantchester for a glass of ale."

"Thank God you stayed. Did you see Bertrand fall in? How exactly did it happen?"

"I'm not altogether sure," replied Radcliffe. He was a tall, well-built man on whom my clothes looked far from comfortable. His own were drying by the fire, deposited there by Mrs Lumley with something approaching religious devotion. "We saw your wife and child a little ahead of us on the towpath, but paid them no particular heed. I was keen to get on back to college, for I've an essay to write for Dr Sutcliffe, and he won't have delays. Tom here wanted to go on to the Lion. He always develops a thirst on our outings."

"But did you see him fall? He's not a careless boy."

"It all happened very quickly, sir. They were quite a few yards ahead of us. Just walking. We'd come to a little before Brasley Bridge. The boy wasn't running or playing or anything, just going along steadily with his mother. I couldn't see clearly how he came to be in the water. But I heard the woman shouting, and when I looked I saw him floundering. That's when I ran up."

"I saw something," broke in Elliot. "Just before the boy fell in. I thought it was a black dog, just behind him. It was nowhere to be seen afterwards, must have run off. But I wonder if it might not have pushed him in. That's funny, though."

I looked curiously at him.

"Funny? In what way?"

"Well, it was a biggish dog, but not the sort to bowl a boy over, or so I should have thought. It was moving oddly, as though it was lame. Almost like a man on all fours. Not much force, you see. Not enough impetus. Like a man sculling with an injury. Still, it must have knocked him in all the same."

I stared at him.

"Yes," I said finally. "You're probably right. It must have knocked him in."

Twenty-Four

W hether as a result of what she had suffered that afternoon, or for reasons I alone could guess, Simone was taken ill again that night. This time, she did not recover by morning. Her fever grew more serious, and when Willingham returned around eight o'clock he expressed real concern about her condition.

"I'm worried about her," he said as he took his leave. "She may have to be moved to Addenbrooke's if things don't improve. Do I have your permission to bring in a colleague for a second opinion? He's a good man, Charlton: you may have heard of him."

Charlton was a professor at the medical school, and, though I had not met him socially, I had often heard his name mentioned with respect. I readily assented to Willingham's suggestion.

Bertrand was making a steady recovery, but was upset to hear that his mother was too ill to visit him. I thought it best not to bring him to her, since the sight of her might set him back.

Around mid-morning, I found time to retire to my study. Willingham had sent in a nurse to look after Simone, and Mrs Lumley was seeing to Bertrand. I would have stayed by Simone's side throughout, but the nurse advised against it, and for my own part I knew there were urgent matters to deal with.

Something in René's letter had intrigued me. The passage he had quoted from the Fleury chronicle had contained the following words: *Abbot Guillaume was thought at first to be a pious man, for his knowledge of the scriptures was unsurpassed, and he spent much of every day immersed in reading of the sacred text.*

Whatever the true state of William's piety, it seemed likely that he not only made a show of being immersed in the Scriptures, but that he was very probably as well read in them as he professed. Scripture may be used to more than one end, and impiety is no barrier to biblical learning. I have seen enough charlatans in my own day, versed in holy utterance from Genesis to Revelation.

Might it not be, I reckoned, that the inscription on William's tomb was no more than a summary of Bible references? There were, after all, other scriptural quotations on the monument. And had not Edward Atherton before his death assembled copious citations on those slips of paper he had inserted into his Bible? Had he too been seeking to disentangle William's cipher?

I spent some time collating Edward's slips, trying to fit them to sections of the inscription, without success. It was as I was about to toss them to one side again that I took note of something I should have seen at the beginning. Edward had written out his biblical quotations, not just in English, but in Latin, the language Abbot William himself would have used. There was nothing remarkable in that. But Edward had, on one or two occasions, gone a step further, and transcribed the Hebrew and Greek originals.

I wondered what possible use this could be. The abbot

was unlikely to have known Hebrew, and his Greek may not have been more than rudimentary. I had, in any case, already endeavoured to make sense of the inscription using Greek as a basis, and had drawn as many blanks as with Latin, French, or English. Hebrew seemed even less likely, given that it used an alphabet yet further removed from that of Latin.

It was then, as I thought about alphabets, that the truth slowly began to dawn, though it was still to take me over an hour before I finally wrestled the conundrum to the ground. My Classics master at school, a stooped man called Runciman (dead these ten years and more), once taught me that Greek, like Hebrew and, I believe, other Eastern alphabets, did not always use simple numbers. The letters of the alphabet themselves might be used for that purpose. Thus, *alpha* might stand for one, *beta* for two and so on, through the tens and hundreds. Latin, with only twenty-one letters, was less well suited to this purpose, but I was sure it could be done.

Excitedly, I turned to one of the letter groups with which I had been struggling: IILCD. This came out as 9:9:10:3:4, a combination that made no sense as a biblical reference. Perhaps I was on the wrong track after all. I tried it all the same, looking up the ninth book of the Bible (which was I Samuel), then its ninth chapter, the tenth verse, and (I was nearer than I thought), the third and fourth words: *Saul ad*. It did not seem promising. And, indeed, as I tried the same method with each of the other letter groups, I came out with as much nonsense as ever, albeit I now had real words to conjure with.

Perhaps it was the sight of actual words that convinced me to plod on. That and the knowledge that, upstairs, Simone was growing more seriously ill. I went up to her from time to time, but the nurse would only bid me be quiet and say she was no better.

A Shadow on the Wall

The final piece of my puzzle fell into place when I looked again at my original transcription of the letters, which I had taken directly from the tomb: BCLDE*LALANTH*OHLELD* OELALDH * OHDMH * QHALHB * IILCD * MHLGC * BMIOBLD *LIMFEI*HBLBLI*OGGDLLA. I noticed something that had seemed insignificant before, but which I had nonetheless preserved as I wrote down the inscription. Some of the letters were joined by a short underline, no more than two at a time. What if these were to be read, not as independent figures, but as groups?

I looked again at my first group: IILCD, which I now wrote down as: IILCD. With a beating heart, I turned again to first Samuel, chapter nine, but this time reading the thirteenth chapter (L and C together making, I assumed, thirteen) and the fourth word: *invenietis*. 'You shall find.' That seemed a great deal more promising.*

It took only minutes after that to assemble the letters into correctly divided groups, and perhaps fifteen minutes after that

---

* This passage may seem a little obscure. Asquith was clearly working at first along the lines of the numerical alphabet known as *abjad*, used even at the present day by the Arabs and Persians. Used in that style, it is relatively simple to assign a value to each letter, for there are twenty-eight letters in the Arabic alphabet, and thirty-two in the Persian. Latin, however, has a mere twenty-one letters from which the cryptographer must work a little differently. Abbot William solved one irksome problem by using lines under letters in order to join them into numerical units, thus LC for thirteen, i.e. ten plus three.

The abbot was, of course, more cunning than this. Each letter (or group of letters) in the coded inscription points, not to letter in the normal text, but to a book of the Bible, a chapter, a verse, or a word.

The Editor

to translate those groups into a connected string of specific Latin words. The grammar left something to be desired, but William's system of encipherment had left him little flexibility. I wrote it all out at last with a shaking hand, and I knew I had found part at least of what I sought.

Ego non sum mortuus, sed vivus; invenietis me ubi dormivi, sub corpus Christi.

It was not difficult to translate, though rather harder to understand:

'I am not dead, but living; you shall find me where I lie, beneath the body of Christ.'

It seemed a platitude; but no one, not even a monk with scholarly pretensions, goes to such pains to wrap a platitude in mystery. The words were individually lifted from Scripture, but the final result was not at all scriptural. William meant something by it, and I intended to find out what that was.

Heartened by my discovery, I went upstairs again to see how Simone was. I found her in as high a fever as ever, breathing hard, and clearly struggling for her life.

"When is Professor Charlton expected?" I asked.

The nurse shook her head. She was a plain-looking local woman of about forty, not very talkative, but, I sensed, efficient and dependable.

"Dr Willingham wasn't sure. He's not certain the professor's in town."

"Is there anything I can do?"

She shook her head again.

"The doctor's done everything he can for the moment. He believes she'll live if she gets through the night."

I looked at her despairingly. Her arms were outside the

covers, and I picked up one hand and held it for a few moments. Her skin was as hot as coals; I almost thought it had left its mark on my palm.

I went downstairs again and fretted. Until Willingham returned, I dared not leave Simone's side. Yet I desperately wanted to get away, to make a final bid to save her life.

An hour later, Willingham arrived with Charlton. The professor had been in London and had only just returned. They barely paused to greet me, but hurried upstairs at once to set about their examination. It took a long time. Bertrand was sleeping in the next room. I sat downstairs, watching the clock and chafing with the most terrible anxiety. It had grown dark outside. A long night lay ahead.

They came down at last, about fifteen minutes later, looking solemn. Charlton, who had barely paused to address me when he entered, now stretched out a hand.

"Professor Asquith," he said. "I'm sorry we should meet under such melancholy circumstances."

"How is my wife?"

"Gravely ill. I must be frank with you. I do not think she will last the night."

"Is there nothing you can do?"

"Very little. Rest assured, I shall do all in my power; but I fear the worst. Hers is not an ordinary fever. Neither Dr Willingham nor I can fathom it."

I looked at Willingham.

"You said you might transfer her to Addenbrooke's. Is that still possible?"

He shook his head.

"Professor Charlton and I have discussed the matter. Her situation has deteriorated since I saw her last. She would not survive the journey. Nor do I think there is much they could do for her there that we cannot as easily do here. Believe me, we intend to exert ourselves fully on her behalf."

"Will you both stay?"

Charlton shook his head.

"I have unavoidable duties at the hospital. But Willingham here knows what to do, and I promise to return when I can during the night."

I hesitated. What I was about to say would, I knew, seem inexplicable to them both, if not the very height of cowardice.

"I cannot stay here," I said. "You will think it infamous of me, but if my wife is to be saved, then I have to be elsewhere tonight. Please forgive me, gentlemen, but I have no choice."

I shall never forget the astonishment and disbelief on their faces. That I should thus desert my dying wife must have seemed to them the gravest moral turpitude. But what else could I do? It would be too late if I waited till morning.

Charlton took his leave shortly after, brusquely, but without retracting his promise to return. I sent Ned to fetch my sister, then went upstairs to see Simone. She did not recognise me. I kissed her forehead softly, then left her with the nurse.

Before leaving, I called on Bertrand. Mrs Lumley was with him. He had woken, and was asking to see his mother.

"Your mother is ill again," I said. "You may see her later if she rallies, but at present she should not be disturbed. The doctor is with her."

"Is that the doctor who was here before?"

"Yes, Dr Willingham. And he brought a colleague with him, Professor Charlton."

"Is he the little man in a black suit?"

"No, the professor's a tall man. He was dressed in grey. Did he call on you?"

Bertrand shook his head.

"I wanted to see *Maman*. I looked into the corridor, but there was a man outside her door. I thought it was the doctor, so I came back in."

"Was this just now?"

"No, it must have been an hour ago."

"You must have been dreaming." I said. "Neither doctor was here then."

"But I saw someone."

"Perhaps it was the nurse."

He shook his head.

"I've seen the nurse," he said. "It wasn't her."

"A friend from college was visiting. Perhaps that was the person you saw. He was wearing a black suit."

"Yes," he said, "that must have been it."

But I think he knew it was a lie, just as I knew he had not been dreaming.

Twenty-Five

My journey to Thornham St Stephen was the most horrific I have ever made or ever hope to make. The night was pitch dark and bitterly cold, and several times I feared to have lost my way in the fens. Halfway there it started to snow, gently at first, then with increasing ferocity, until I despaired of arriving at my destination at all. Had it not been for my horse, whose sense of the road was unerring, I should certainly have strayed across open ground and very possibly have paid with my life for my foolhardy actions.

I arrived at the village just as the evening service was drawing to a close. Guided by the lights in the church, I headed there directly. It was still snowing heavily, and I was reluctant to leave my horse and the dogcart outside. I guessed, however, that everyone would be at church, even on such a night, and that going there would be my quickest way of finding someone to stable her.

I slipped inside and took a seat in a back pew, remaining there through the remainder of the service, a matter of some ten minutes. As the worshippers filed out, I caught sight of Mrs O'Reilly. Beckoning her aside, I asked if she would stable my horse.

"Will you need a room for the night, sir?"

"I don't think so. I shall want to get back to Cambridge once I've finished my business here."

"I'll make up a bed for you all the same, sir. You may not be able to leave Thornham if this snow holds."

"Very well. But I may arrive late at the inn."

"No matter, sir. What are inns for? Come as late as you please. By the way, sir, have you seen anything of Dr Atherton, the old rector's brother?"

"Matthew?" I thought it best to conceal the truth. "I saw him a few days ago. He was very well. He sends his best wishes to you, and asks particularly after your Irish stew and – what was it?"

"Champ, sir. I can make some for you tonight, if you need to fill your stomach."

"That's very generous of you. I may take you up on your offer. Now, I think the Reverend Lethaby is waiting."

She hurried out through the west door, and I followed at a slower pace. Lethaby had been shaking hands with his parishioners, bidding them good-night with the patronising air common in churchmen of his temperament. His eyes widened with far from good-natured surprise when he caught sight of me approaching from the empty church. It took several moments before he recovered himself sufficiently to re-invent his unctuous smile.

"Professor Asquith! Goodness gracious. I had no idea you were in the congregation."

"I came in at the end. I was sorry to have missed your sermon."

"There was little to miss. I keep my preaching short on a Sunday evening. A brief homily on the follies of socialism. But what on earth brings you to Thornham on a night like this?"

"My wife is dying, Mr Lethaby. She is in the grip of a fever from which the doctors do not expect her to recover. They think she may not last the night."

"Good heavens, you leave me quite speechless. I did not even know you were married. How did this tragedy happen?"

"I think you know that as well as I. I'm here to put an end to this thing. But I cannot do it without your help."

The expression of professional sympathy on his face collapsed at once into one of sullen defiance.

"I think it would be better if you left, Professor. We've had this out before. I've told you what I think."

"You know I can't do that. If I don't stop him, his depredations will continue. Are you prepared to have the weight of that on your soul?"

"I mean you no harm, Professor. But I cannot permit—"

"Permit? Who are you to permit or ban? It is not within your authority."

"The bishop—"

"The bishop is in Ely. He will not come here tonight, he need know nothing of what passes here. Not he, not the dean, not the entire chapter."

"I cannot act without—"

"If you do not act, others will die. Edward Atherton is dead. His mother is dead. And now Matthew Atherton is missing."

His face turned grey. I had expected a longer struggle of the sort I had encountered previously, but something seemed to have happened to Lethaby in the meantime. He tried to put up a show. His face worked for several moments, searching for an expression to suit a stouter rebuff, but he had no heart for it. His collapse, when it came, was complete.

"Very well, Asquith. What is it you want me to do?"

"I want to start by opening William de Lindesey's tomb again."

"Out of the question. Apart from other considerations, it would take several men."

"What became of the equipment used to lift the lid?"

"Cowper took it back to his yard after his men put the lid straight again."

"Has no one in the village tackle of the kind?"

"I dare say the blacksmith . . ."

"Then we shall go to him. Has your churchwarden left yet?"

He shook his head.

"Albert stays on till the church is shut. He'll be here somewhere."

"Let's find him, then. If he'll lend a hand, we can have this done in a trice."

We ran Albert Ryman to earth in the vestry, where he had settled down with a bottle of 'something against the cold'. It was, I think, how he best liked to spend a Sunday evening. He was not well pleased to be told of my plan, and at first refused to have anything to do with it. I remembered that it had been he who had opened the door of the rectory bedroom and found Edward Atherton in that terrible condition. The poor man could scarcely be blamed for his reluctance. But that evening Simone's life was more precious to me than anything, certainly more than Albert Ryman's sensibilities. I told him why I had come, and I told him what would happen to us – all of us – should I not succeed. I had scarcely finished when he hared off to the blacksmith's as though the devil himself was driving him.

"What has happened since my last visit?" I asked Lethaby once we were alone.

Now that he was in the vestry, he busied himself in putting away his vestments. He had already hung up his chasuble and stole. As I spoke, he was untying the strings of his amice, and I noticed that his fingers fumbled at the knots.

"There have been some deaths in the parish," he murmured, visibly unhappy to be forced to this disclosure. "More than there should have been. A number of children have died, and the doctor thinks that if there are others the authorities will have to be informed." He paused, removing the amice and folding it. It went on to a shelf next to his maniple.

"Another child fell ill yesterday," he said. "His mother was with me today. We said prayers for him at both morning and evening services. A farmer's child called Dan Piggott."

"Another choirboy?"

He nodded glumly.

"Yes, as a matter of fact. All the dead children sang in the choir. It seemed mere coincidence at first, then evidence of contamination. We suspended the choir a few months ago, but the illnesses have continued."

"There is contamination here," I said, "but not of the physical variety."

He told me more of how Thornham St Stephen had suffered, and admitted that, for some weeks now, he had been attempting to exorcise the spirit of William de Lindesey.

"I pray in here night and day," he said, "but it makes no difference."

"Prayer alone will not suffice. There is something else that must be done first."

"What is that?"

I hesitated.

"Let us wait until we've looked inside the tomb."

"Why do you need to do that?"

"I'm looking for something," I said.

I told him of the inscription, and my decipherment of it.

"But surely there's never been any question of where

William de Lindesey was buried," Lethaby observed. "The inscription must mean something else."

"I agree. But until I've opened the tomb again, I cannot be certain."

At that moment, Ryman returned, accompanied by a huge man in a heavy coat who was introduced to us as Harry Stanton, the blacksmith. Big man though he was, Harry was plainly terrified to be brought to the church for such an undertaking.

We went back into the main body of the church, a dark shell lit only by candles. Ryman and the blacksmith together wheeled a heavily laden barrow down to the chancel, setting it down with a very final bump next to William de Lindesey's tomb.

The tarpaulin had been removed, and the lid set square again as Lethaby had already told me. Stanton said he would set up the equipment, but that nothing would induce him to remain while we opened the tomb. He had heard what had happened to Ezekiel Finch on the occasion of the tomb's first opening, and would not be persuaded that the same thing or worse would not happen now.

His refusal put new heart into Ryman, who now put in his own objections.

"At least set up the equipment for us," I said, "and show us what to do."

There was some quibbling, but in the end they agreed. I looked at my watch. It was almost eight o'clock. How long would Simone take to die if things continued as they were? Was she dead already? I dared not let myself think like that.

It took the two men some time to set up the trestles and winch. Stanton's equipment was not really designed to move heavy stone, only to lift carts and pieces of farm machinery, and even as he erected it he expressed reservations about its suitability.

"I don't think it'll hold, Reverend," he muttered at one point. "That lid's heavier than anything I've ever lifted in the smithy. The whole thing could come collapsing down, as 'twere."

Lethaby looked at me, almost relieved by this prediction of impending failure. Perhaps I would even now abandon my scheme.

"Mr Stanton," I asked, "do you have children?"

"Five young ones, sir. The oldest is twelve."

"Any that sing in the choir?"

I saw his face turn pale beneath the surface ruddiness of the skin. He knew what I was driving at.

"When choir was together, yes, sir. Ezra and Jude, sir. Bible names. Reverend will tell you my wife is constant at church, sir. She chose all their names from the good book."

"Mr Stanton, you know that some choirboys have already died. You must be worried about your two boys. Then let me tell you why I've come here tonight."

I made no tales up, but spoke to him directly, telling him what fate might await his children and others if we could not lay William de Lindesey to his eternal rest – or eternal punishment. He listened without so much as a shake of his head, like a great silent beast giving ear to the herdsman's voice. When I had finished, he simply nodded. He would help us.

"What about you, Albert?" Lethaby asked his churchwarden.

Betrayed by his neighbour, Albert caved in.

We started work together now, under Stanton's directions. His strength was formidable. While the rest of us kept things steady, he hauled on the ropes to raise the lid and slip it beneath rollers.

But for the sound of our working, the chancel was unnaturally quiet. The heavy snowfall muffled all sounds from outside, and it felt as though the world had been taken away completely. All that was left to us was the dark church, and even that was circumscribed. Ryman had brought large candles from the vestry, and we had set them around the tomb, in order to illuminate our work. A few others continued to burn in other parts of the church, lighting a lectern here and a carving there. Otherwise, we were in the deepest darkness, conscious of the mass of stone about us, and the vastness of the roof, soaring high above us.

The lid rolled back slowly, and though a dark odour rose from within, no one cried out or fainted. We paused at one point, and a great silence fell, and then, before we could fall to work again, there was a sound out in the shadows, not far away. Something was shuffling across the flagstones.

"It's all right," I said. "Go on with your work. Nothing will harm you."

Stanton and Ryman were sweating, less from physical exertion, I thought, then fear. I could feel my own heart beating horridly, and when I looked at Lethaby he was as pale as the light in which he stood.

"Take this," I said, passing a sheet of paper to Lethaby.

"What is it?"

"A formula of excommunication. It dates from the tenth century. I want you to read it aloud."

"But surely you can—"

"No. You are a priest."

I remembered William's challenge to me that night in the rectory: *Thou nart a prest. Thou hast noon auctoritee over me.*

"Will this be enough?"

I shook my head.

"It will do no more than hold him back. There is something here stronger than you. It must be destroyed."

The dragging sound continued. No one moved. Lethaby unfolded the paper with a shaking hand.

"It's in Latin," he said.

"Just read it," I told him.

"In nomine patris," he began, *"et filii et virtute spiritus sancti necnon auctoritate episcopis per Petrum principem apostolorum divinitus collata, a sanctae matris ecclesiae gremio segregamus ac perpetuae maledictionis anathemate condemnamus . . ."*

The shuffling stopped abruptly.

"Keep on," I told the men. "It will stay back."

They hesitated, then set to work again. The sound of the stone being rolled back mingled with that of Lethaby's voice intoning the malediction. One candle flickered and went out, as though snuffed by an invisible hand. I went to it and lit it again. Another was extinguished, then another. Lethaby continued to read, moving from one candle to the next, while I followed him, relighting them.

"That's as far as it's safe to take it, sir," said Stanton.

"Thank you," I said.

Lethaby's voice faltered and died away. He had come to the end of the formula.

"Should I read it a second time?"

"Not unless it starts up again. Come over here. Bring a couple of candles with you."

He joined me at the side of the tomb and handed me one of the candles. I looked at my watch. Just after nine o'clock. Was Simone still alive? And Bertrand – had he fallen ill yet?

I raised the candle, and together Lethaby and I brought light to the inside of the tomb.

I am not sure what I expected to see. Bones, perhaps, or a mound of dust. Certainly not what was lying there at the bottom of the tomb.

Lethaby uttered an ejaculation and stepped back, almost stumbling against the trestle. I remained fixed there, unable to pull myself away. I made no sound, I did not move for a long time. Lethaby stood watching me, his candle trembling in his hand.

"Who is it?" he asked at last, and his voice seemed small and trembling like the candle flame he held.

"Matthew Atherton," I said as I stepped away from the tomb. The body lying there was lacerated like nothing I had ever seen, but the face had been untouched. There could be no mistake. I looked up at the shadows and felt them press down on me like naked stone.

Twenty-Six

W hen I had recovered myself sufficiently, I returned to the tomb and looked inside again. The face of Matthew Atherton, twisted into an expression of frank horror, stared up at me, but it was not him I sought. I moved the candle from side to side, peering sharply into every corner. As far as I could tell, Atherton's body was alone. What I had come for was not there.

Desperate now, for I was certain I had lost Simone, I looked up at Lethaby.

"It isn't there," I mumbled. I had come to some sort of end, yet I could not come to terms with it.

"Tell me what it is you're looking for."

I raised the candle to see him more closely. He was standing with Stanton and Ryman, watching me as though they thought I might have been personally responsible for transporting Matthew Atherton to that terrible place.

"A relic," I said. "A small statue in the shape of a seated man, perhaps with a goat's head. It was brought to de Lindesey when he was Abbot of Thornham. I am convinced that all his strength for evil resides in it. We have to find it and render it harmless."

"And you think de Lindesey's inscription points the way?"

I shrugged.

"I thought it might have done. Now, I'm less sure."

"What exactly did it say again?"

"'I am not dead, but living; you shall find me where I lie, beneath the body of Christ.'"

"You think it refers to this relic?"

"I don't know what else it can mean. The relic was precious to him, and we know he travelled with it as far as France. There's no record of it after his death. The inscription on his tomb makes no sense if it simply refers to his own remains. But it may have been intended as a clue to anyone after him who wished to know the location of the statue."

"Then perhaps they have already found it. The relic may have been removed hundreds of years ago."

I admitted it was a possibility that had already crossed my own mind. But if the relic had indeed been buried with William de Lindesey, it was hard to see how anyone could have found it before this without drawing attention to the fact that his tomb had been reopened. To my knowledge, there was no record of such a task having been undertaken.

"You say this statue was a relic?" Lethaby asked.

"Possibly. It was certainly treated as one. I think it may in reality have been some sort of pagan fetish from the Middle East. It makes little difference."

"Perhaps not." Lethaby looked round nervously into the shadows. Since he had stopped reading the malediction, the silence had grown menacing again. "But remember that relics used to be deposited in altar stones."

I stared at him. How could I have been so obtuse?

"Beneath the . . . the Body of Christ," I stammered. "The consecrated host."

He nodded, then glanced round again. A muffled sound came from the shadows to his right.

"How many altars are there in this church?"

"Seven," he answered.

"We'll try the high altar first."

He looked at me as if I had suggested setting fire to the church.

"That's out of the question," he said. "I wonder you can even think of it. It would be an act of sacrilege to dismantle the altar."

"What do you call that thing out there?" I shouted. "Isn't that sacrilege enough for you?"

"You can go to Ely tomorrow and obtain a dispensation. I'll travel with you, we'll present the case together."

"Tomorrow will be too late. My wife will be dead." In my new-found hope, I thrust from me the thought that Simone might already be past all help.

"I'm truly sorry, but the altar is sacred. I can't let you desecrate it."

He turned to Ryman and Stanton, who were standing nervously a few yards away, as though ready to take to their heels the moment they saw or heard anything untoward.

"You men," Lethaby ordered. "I want you to take Professor Asquith from the church. What he is planning is sacrilege. Don't hurt him, but make sure he is put out and kept out."

The two villagers looked at one another awkwardly. Ryman, more accustomed to the ways of the church, spoke up.

"I'm not rightly sure, Rector. That sounds like police work to me. I'm not sure as we could do it with a conscience."

"Didn't you hear me?" Lethaby's voice began to grow shrill. The fear was blunting his powers of self-control. "I want him out now. See to it."

Had he been a liked man, had he ingratiated himself with the people of his parish as much as with Sir Philip Ousby, perhaps Lethaby's orders might have been heeded. I know I could not have resisted a man as strong as Stanton, even had I had a weapon to hand. But the rector had undermined his own authority by his brusqueness, and neither Stanton nor Ryman was going to get dragged into a quarrel for his sake.

"Come on," said Stanton to his friend. "I reckon the rector should see to church affairs hisself."

The two men turned and, without another word, hurried out of the chancel and down the nave. They were gone from sight in moments, and I only knew they had gone when the west door slammed shut with a crash.

Lethaby and I remained in the darkness. The shuffling sound had started again, louder now, and more insistent.

"For God's sake," I urged him, "read the malediction again."

"It's too late for that," he said. "It's out of my hands now. We should leave and close the church, just like Edward Atherton tried to do. I should have done it months ago."

I shook my head. What he proposed was monstrous.

"I will not leave this place without attempting what I came to do. Are you willing to help me or not?"

He looked at me once, then cast a glance in the direction from which the shuffling came.

"You must find your own salvation," he hissed. He crossed himself once, then turned and followed the others. His footsteps rang out loudly on the stone floor, quick and echoing all the way. At last, the great door slammed again, followed by the sound of a heavy bolt as Lethaby rammed it home.

I was alone at last with what I feared most in the world. For the first time since entering the church, I noticed how very cold it was. My breath hung in a white cloud in front of the candle next to me, and vanished, and reappeared.

I looked away, and there, beneath the east window, I caught sight of two candles still burning on the altar, and a steady light before the host. My mind was made up.

I walked slowly to the altar rail. It ran the full width of the chancel, but at the centre a small gate had been inserted to allow the priest passage. I drew back the bolt and pushed the gate open. Behind me, a new sound started in the darkness: measured footsteps in the nave, now fading, now growing strong again, and again fading.

"Lethaby, is that you?" I called, thinking he had returned. There was no answer. Again the sound of footsteps, again silence. "Ryman? Stanton? Are you there?" Still no answer. I peered into the shadows, but could see no one. Steeling myself, I turned my back on the body of the church and stepped through the gate.

The altar was still decked with the Eucharist plate. Hurrying now, I cleared it away – a large cross, two enormous gilded candlesticks, a gold chalice, a platen, and two silver cruets. A long embroidered frontal hung down the face of the altar. I tore it away, and pulled off the altar cloth. Beneath lay a large rectangular stone block topped by a *mensa*, a thin marble slab running its entire length.

The marble was too heavy for me to move unaided. I exerted all my strength, but it simply would not budge. My heart sank, all my hopes, faint as they were, cheated by this last, unexpected obstacle. Behind me, the shuffling sound suddenly quickened.

I looked about me in desperation. On the floor beside me stood the candlesticks, which I had left there to provide me with a little light. There was still a chance. I removed the candle from one and lifted the stick. It must have weighed at least thirty pounds, and though it could be gripped easily enough by its stem, it was rendered extremely unwieldy by its large base. I am not by any means a strong man, but fear and pity lent me the strength I needed.

I raised the stick and brought it down, base first, upon centre of the marble. Again and again I hefted it, bringing it crashing down on the same spot, and at the fourth or fifth blow I heard a cracking sound. I raised the candlestick again, and this time when it smashed against the slab, the stone broke in a single ragged fissure across its entire width.

Even halved, the marble was hard to shift. I managed to insert a hand into the gap opened at the centre, and by hard pushing widened it until I had the whole thing moving. A little further, and it dropped over the edge, striking the floor with a sharp crash that echoed through the church.

I turned and took the candle from the second stick. Turning back to the altar, I held it low over the stone. In the centre, flanked by four consecration crosses, was a square hole that had been excavated from the bare rock. Inside the hole lay a large bundle wrapped in embroidered silk cloth. I reached inside and lifted the whole thing. The cloth had rotted and fell away in strips at my touch, but the object it contained was perfectly solid and quite heavy.

With shaking hands I tore at what was left of the fabric. It dropped to the ground, revealing what lay beneath. Eyes stared out at me, then I distinguished the shape of a monstrous head, inhuman, satanic. The next moment I recognised it: I had seen one like it before, in the Fitzwilliam Museum. A wooden statue of the ram-headed Egyptian god Knum, his twisting horns and long ears branching from an elongated head. In that dim light it seemed to me the very embodiment of evil.

There was a sound behind me. This time I turned.

Half in darkness, half in light, a hooded figure stood at

the foot of the altar steps watching me, a thing of shadow, yet shadow married to substance. I saw very little of it, and nothing of its face, yet one thing impressed itself on me and will never leave my dreams, and that was the hand that emerged from the wide-necked sleeve. It was a hand neither of flesh nor of bone, but somewhere between, with the look of ashes about it, as though it had been burned and then monstrously regrown.

He stood there like everything I had ever feared, misshapen, silent, and reeking of malice. The church was filled with the stench of him and the atmosphere of menace that followed in his wake.

I began to recite what little I could remember of the malediction I had given Lethaby to read, but I had no heart in it. I was not a priest, I had no authority. My voice faltered and the words fell from me like dead leaves from a tree. I looked at the abbot, not knowing what he might do, knowing only that he was too powerful for me. As I did so, my eye was caught by a slight movement to his left. On the ground beside him, something dark and misshapen had started crawling towards me.

At that moment, I heard a voice behind me, a man's voice, pleasant and relaxed, yet somehow insistent. He was speaking words I knew well, the liturgy for the dead from the Anglican Book of Common Prayer. I turned and looked behind me. Near the altar stood a barely visible figure. I cannot say for sure, but I did think then that he was dressed in the clothes of a priest.

I stepped quickly back to the altar and, raising the statue in both hands, brought it crashing down on the side of the stone. It split into dozens of pieces, and I did not have to strike with it again.

There was a great cry behind me, and every candle in the

church was snuffed out, leaving me in the most absolute blackness. The cold, which had been intense, grew deeper and more bitter still. A terrible wind rushed through the darkness, knocking me down against the side of the altar. I lifted my head and tried to rise, but the darkness bewildered me. The last thing I remember is hearing my name called out again and again, then silence, then nothing.

Twenty-Seven

They tell me I was ill for two months afterwards. I know nothing of that. Mrs O'Reilly kept me in the room she had made ready at the inn, and the local doctor came to visit me there.

My first memory is that of opening my eyes on a morning in early spring to see Simone's face gazing down at me anxiously. I remember thinking first that it was the next morning, and then that everything had been a dream. Only gradually did I come to understand the truth.

In spite of the smile, there were tears in Simone's eyes. When I looked more closely, she seemed older than when I had last seen her. Her own illness had left deep scars, and the weeks of anxiety, when she did not know whether I would live or die, had exacted an even greater toll.

"You were very unfair," she said. "You left me in Cambridge dying, then I got better, then a telegram came from this place saying you were ill."

The doctors allowed me to go home three days later. Mrs O'Reilly bade me a tearful farewell and asked me to keep in touch, to let her know how I was faring. When I offered her payment for her board and lodging, she refused, and when I persisted, she grew angry.

"None of us here knows rightly just what has happened in

A Shadow on the Wall

Thornham, but we all reckons as we have a lot to thank you for, sir. I've been speakin' with Albert Ryman, and he's told me a bit of what went on that night in the church. Whatever you did, sir, it's been quiet round here since."

"Quiet?"

"Ever since the old rector died, folk have heard things at night. And some have seen things, things I'd as soon not talk about. But since that night all's been much as it was. Our days and nights are quiet again, sir. And your good self apart, no one's fallen ill since then neither. Or died for that matter."

"I'm heartily glad to hear it, Mrs O'Reilly. Tell me, did you hear or see anything yourself?"

Her face paled, and she nodded.

"Yes, sir. More than once, sir, I seen it. I'd as soon not talk about it, sir."

"I understand. And you say all is as it should be now?"

"Yes, sir."

"I pray it stays so."

I have never been back to Thornham St Stephen. Mrs O'Reilly writes to me from time to time, telling me how the village is faring. The new rector has got the choir back together, and they are in finer voice than ever. He is a good man, she says, and dines with Sir Philip only once a year. The new altar is a proper wooden affair, built of oak, and backed by a magnificent East Anglian painted retable found by the rector in the church loft. The wicked abbot's tomb is still there, but sealed with mortar now. The rector has ordered it festooned with flowers every Easter.

Bertrand sings in the choir at King's, and his English improves by leaps and bounds. I am writing this for him, so that one day he will understand.

Simone expects our first child in the autumn. She is certain it will be a girl. I am less sure. The nursery is being painted as I write. Simone's fever broke at about the time I must have been at the altar in St Stephen's Church, and she recovered rapidly from that moment. Dr Willingham described the change in her condition rather lightly as 'bordering on the miraculous'. I merely smiled and said he might be closer to the truth than he thought. He believes I went to Thornham St Stephen to pray, and he is content to let me think my prayers took effect. I shall never tell him or anyone but my wife and children the truth.

I have since examined statues of Knum in both the Fitzwilliam here and the British Museum. They differ in size and colouring one from the other, but all bear a close resemblance to the one that William de Lindesey hid in the altar next to his tomb. James Hallam-Pierce, a Fellow of my college and an expert on the crusades, tells me such an object might have found its way from Egypt to Syria, and thence into the hands of a crusading knight.

I cannot imagine the statue had any power for evil or good in itself. It was an idol, nothing more. But if William and others had invested it with their warped longings and dreams of immortality, then it will have acted as a focus for their every evil thought and deed. It is gone now. Albert Ryman found the fragments of rotten wood scattered about the altar, and burned them unceremoniously at the back of the church. The altar was reconsecrated, and prayers said in the church and throughout the village.

There is a little churchyard not far from Wilburton, where Matthew Atherton is buried next to his mother, her body having been re-interred there after a short spell in the churchyard at Ely. I travel there as often as I can, to lay flowers on his grave and pray that he find rest. How he came to be laid in William de Lindesey's tomb, and how he died are questions I prefer not to dwell on. The police showed some interest in the matter to begin with, but even they had, in the end, to recognise the impossibility of ever reaching a proper conclusion.

I visited Atherton's grave last week, on a Sunday afternoon, as I am accustomed to, and found that a headstone had been erected there at last. The sexton told me it had been paid for by a nephew who lives in Peterborough, a man I have never met. It is a fine stone, matching his mother's beside it. Beneath Atherton's name and the dates of his birth and death are inscribed the words: 'Fellow of Sidney Sussex College, Cambridge', and underneath that there is part of a verse of Scripture, from the Book of Job.

He shall return out of darkness.

I have said nothing to Simone about the inscription. After all, the nephew is innocent of the matters I have just related, and his choice of the passage can have had no other motive than the obvious. Nonetheless, I have not slept well since reading it. Yesterday, Mrs Lumley told me there are rats in the attic. She has heard them at night.